The Fire Giant

Handersen Publishing, LLC
Lincoln, Nebraska

Giant Series Book #3

The Fire Giant

This book is a work of fiction. All characters and other incidents are a product of the author's imagination, and locales are used in a fictitious manner. Any resemblance to actual events, or persons, living or dead, is entirely coincidental.

Manufactured in the United States of America.

Library of Congress Cataloging-in-Publication Data
Names: Spudich, Giulietta M., author.
Title: The fire giant / Giulietta M. Spudich.
Description: Lincoln, Nebraska : Handersen Publishing, LLC, [2023] | Series: Giant series ; 3 | Audience: Ages 9-12. | Audience: Grades 4-6. | Summary: "In a small town in Mexico, Lupita must find a way to honor the spirit living in the volcano, control her new found fire powers, and save her village with the help of her friend Carlos"-- Provided by publisher.
Identifiers: LCCN 2023000759 (print) | LCCN 2023000760 (ebook) | ISBN 9781647031060 (paperback) | ISBN 9781947854994 (hardback) | ISBN 9781647031077 (ebook)
Subjects: CYAC: Ability--Fiction. | Anger--Fiction. | Volcanoes--Fiction.| Mexico--Fiction. | Fantasy. | LCGFT: Fantasy fiction. | Novels.
Classification: LCC PZ7.1.S71784 Fi 2023 (print)|LCC PZ7.1.S71784 (ebook) | DDC [Fic]--dc23
LC record available at https://lccn.loc.gov/2023000759
LC ebook record available at https://lccn.loc.gov/2023000760

Author Website: www.ElementGirls.org
Publisher Website: www.HandersenPublishing.com
Publisher Email: editors@HandersenPublishing.com

The Fire Giant

Giulietta M. Spudich

Handersen Publishing, LLC
Lincoln, Nebraska

Chapter
One

Tapping her pencil on unfinished math homework, Lupita gazed out the living room window. The volcano loomed over the low roofs of her city in Southwest Mexico. It stood taller than even the cathedral's stone towers. To get to the volcano, her family would have to drive over rolling hills of pine, oak and huge parota trees to where it stood on the coast overlooking the ocean. It only took twenty minutes in the car. But they had not been there for years.

Lupita wished she was there now, splashing in the waves on this warm day. All her life, when she played in the sea, the volcano stood above her like a comforting, ancient protector. But this year the volcano often spit smoke into the sky and shook the ground, knocking Lupita's corn husk dolls to the floor. She got the feeling the volcano was angry. And she wondered why.

The volcano was calm right now. She had math homework to finish. She turned to the notebook in front of her.

Her little brother Bernardo interrupted her by running into the house with mud all over his legs.

"Goal!" he yelled and kicked a dirt-covered ball to the table where Lupita sat. It brushed her shin.

"Bernardo!" she said in a tight voice, wanting to yell. Mud stained her sock. But Abuela, Mama's grandmother, was sleeping in the hammock in the corner.

"Shh!" Lupita said with a finger to her lips.

Bernardo covered his mouth but still ran around the room kicking the ball. He kicked it past the sofa, knocked the table leg and scraped a chair to rescue it. How Abuela could sleep through it, Lupita didn't know.

Abuela was so old that she was ancient. She stopped speaking a year ago, around the time their volcano got more active. Sometimes Abuela wrote, but it was hard with her arthritis. She hardly ever cooked anymore.

Now Abuela was too tired to do much but sleep. Lupita missed her. They had always been friends.

"Bernardo!" Mama's voice sailed out of the kitchen. "Is that awful noise you?"

Mama appeared at the archway between the kitchen and living room. Her red apron had a chili pepper on it, and the words "Sweet and Spicy." She had a spicy expression on her face.

"No playing ball in the house," Mama scolded. "Go clean up, we eat soon!"

"I'm starving!" Bernardo exclaimed, kicking the ball up the stairs.

All this noise was not helping Lupita finish her homework. She propped her elbows on the living room table that doubled as a desk and a place to eat. The numbers in the equations swam.

Lupita took a sip of horchata. The sweet, smooth rice milk soothed her throat while the cinnamon woke her up. Even though it was nice and thick, it wasn't food. Her empty stomach rumbled. She wasn't allowed to snack before dinner. It wasn't fair.

Lupita had lost her lunch to Nilda again.

Thinking about the school bully made Lupita's head swim with anger. That wouldn't help with math.

Lupita blinked to focus on the problem. The equations started to make more sense to her. She had just started writing a solution when Papa came in the front door. His boots made stomping noises as he passed through the living room and greeted Mama in the kitchen.

They started having a loud discussion about whether or not to buy a new dishwasher.

Lupita dropped her pencil with a 'clack' on the table. It was hopeless. Math wasn't going to happen today.

Lupita met eyes with her great-grandmother, who was finally awake. Abuela's eyes were dark like Lupita's and set in a face filled with deep lines.

Lupita rolled her eyes against all the chaos and covered her ears with her hands. She thought she saw a glimmer of laughter in Abuela's face.

"Lupita!" Mama said, appearing in the kitchen doorway holding a wooden spoon covered with sauce. "Did you finish your homework?"

"No, but – " Lupita wanted to explain that it was too loud to concentrate.

"You must finish your homework in time for dinner," Mama said. "Thirty minutes!"

Lupita tried to focus. If math homework stopped her from eating dinner on time, she'd be so angry. She could almost feel steam coming out of her ears.

Lupita picked up her eraser. What she had written was completely wrong, she saw that now. Just as she finished erasing, the ground trembled under her feet. Her pencil clattered onto the floor. A column of smoke poured into the sky from the volcano's mouth.

This happened almost every day. Even though the little earthquake was already over, her concentration had been broken. Again.

"I can't take this!" Lupita yelled.

It was almost like the anger of the volcano entered her, then. Heat built up in her belly and warmed her face. She stood up, pushed her chair out with an awful scraping noise and glared at her math homework.

The corner of her notebook caught fire.

"What?" Lupita said aloud.

She grabbed the glass of horchata and threw it onto the flames. The liquid messed up all her answers, dissolving them into a gray smudge.

Lupita's whole body tensed. Her heart beat rapidly and her face felt hot.

How did her math homework suddenly catch on fire?

Abuela stared at Lupita from her hammock, her deep, dark eyes like infinite pools that knew everything.

Chapter
Two

Lupita shifted in the too-small chair in the classroom. Her thighs touched the top of her desk. Why did all the desks have to be the same tiny size?

The slide on the screen showed a black and white photo. People were walking up the volcano in a long line. The women wore dresses with full skirts that reached down to their ankles. Each had a flower in her hand.

It was a familiar photo – one they had at home. She tuned in to her teacher.

"In the early 1900s, red flowers and ears of corn were offered to the volcano," Mr. Gonzalez explained. "This ceremony was done every year to calm the volcano. But we have forgotten our customs and traditions these days."

Lupita thought Mr. Gonzalez looked sad. His mouth turned down.

After a sigh, Mr. Gonzalez continued, "Some of you have relatives in this very photo. Lupita, I believe this is one of your ancestors?"

Lupita blinked and cringed as the eyes of the other students turned to her.

Mr. Gonzalez pointed at the slide. A woman stood at the top of the line of people, near the crater. She wore a long, white dress with a dark shawl hanging down. A little girl in a similar outfit stood close to her.

Though the woman's face was turned away, Lupita knew who it was.

"Great-great-grandmother Nayeli," she said, her voice whisper-thin. Sweat beaded on her forehead. She wished the students would stop staring at her.

"Would you like to say anything about the ceremony?" Mr. Gonzalez asked. "Any stories passed down in your family?"

Though Mama never liked to talk about Nayeli, Abuela told stories about her. At least, Abuela used to tell the old stories, back when she spoke.

Every year, Nayeli would lead the people of their small town up the volcano. They would each lay a red flower and an ear of corn by the crater and thank the volcano for protecting the city. The flowers grew in Nayeli's very own garden. Lupita lived in the same house as her ancestors. The old bush still grew, with thin branches and spiky leaves, but it didn't flower anymore.

Lupita didn't want to say anything about Nayeli or the flowers. With everyone staring, her voice would come out all shaky. Then everyone would laugh and tease her about her size, about her shyness.

Her armpits sweat, and she didn't even want to move in case the stains were seen.

So she shook her head no.

Giggles reached her ears. She looked away from a cluster of girls and met eyes with Carlos.

Carlos was a shy boy. They met when they were five years old. He was the smallest kid in the class, and she was the largest. It kind of made them the same.

Mr. Gonzalez frowned. He flipped to the next slide, which had four pictures of volcanoes with the words 'extinct', 'dormant', 'active' and 'erupting' under each. He pointed to the third volcano.

"Our volcano was dormant. Now it is clearly active," he said. "In fact, it has become very active in the last year. Some scientists classify it as erupting."

A few kids made explosion noises and threw up their hands.

Lupita tensed and she swallowed hard. She didn't want to think about explosions or fire. Math homework erupting into flames was scary. She shook her head to forget about it. Hopefully it was just one of those weird things that would never, ever happen again.

It was time to eat. Mr. Gonzalez came over to Lupita's desk as the other kids packed up their stuff and left the room for the lunchroom.

"Lupita, I'd love to hear more about your family history," Mr. Gonzalez said. "I'm sure your classmates would like it too."

She shrugged. Her jaw was tight. Mr. Gonzalez was nice. But he didn't know the other kids. She didn't want to be teased.

"Your essays are always very interesting. You clearly know a lot about the history of this city," Mr. Gonzalez said. "Think about sharing more with us, please?" He smiled a little.

She smiled back, because she knew that's what he wanted. But it hurt her jaw.

"Have a good lunch," he said. He left the room, swinging his briefcase.

Once he was gone, Nilda came over. Like always.

It's not like Nilda could beat Lupita up. Lupita was bigger after all. But something happened when Nilda's eyes narrowed and she showed her teeth. Lupita felt weak and sweaty.

"Well," Nilda said, looming over Lupita's desk. "You know what I want."

Carlos gave Lupita a sad look from the doorway, near the colorful serape blanket hanging on the wall.

Lupita clamped her teeth together. Every day it was the same. Every day Lupita hoped it wouldn't happen. But every day, it did.

Lupita put her lunch money into Nilda's sweaty palm.

"Not like you need to eat more!" Nilda said, walking swiftly out of the room, her head held high.

Carlos slid across the floor to her. "You can have one of my taquitos," he offered.

"Thanks, Carlos," Lupita said. Though she loved the crispy, deep-fried taquitos Carlos' mom made, she felt bad about taking his food. But he wouldn't take 'no' for an answer.

She gathered up her papers, stuffed them in her backpack and followed her best friend out of the room.

Carlos and Lupita sat in the outdoor section of the canteen. The warm wind brought scents of flowers. The canteen was covered, so it was nice and shady. Carlos' taquito was delicious but small. Lupita's hungry stomach moaned.

Chin in hand, she looked out at the volcano. No smoke today.

"What do you think the volcano would do?" Lupita asked Carlos.

Carlos gave her a puzzled look, his eyebrows pinched in towards each other.

"I mean if someone took its lunch money," Lupita said.

"I think it would erupt," Carlos said. His soft gaze fixed on Lupita.

"Me too," Lupita replied. She stared at the volcano again.

"Lupita?" Carlos asked. "Are you thinking you should erupt at Nilda?"

"Yes," Lupita said. "That's exactly what I am thinking. But I don't know how."

Chapter
Three

School was over, and Lupita was walking home. Palm trees lined the little park. Though there was a breeze, the hot sun baked her. Her stomach was counting the minutes before she got home. The thought of a tasty snack made her mouth water.

The volcano spewed white smoke into the vivid blue sky. Maybe it was angry, like she was. She kicked another rock out of her way.

"I'm sick of Nilda!" she yelled at the smoking volcano. Wisps of white continued to curl from its mouth.

Lupita kicked a foot-sized stone and felt her

toe jam. She cried out. She had to limp the last few streets home.

She dumped her backpack by the door and went straight to the kitchen. Mama was stirring a pot. The smell of pinto beans and jalapeno peppers greeted Lupita's senses.

"Lupita, could you get your brother?" Mama asked. "He's been playing ball all afternoon and he needs to do his homework now."

"OK," Lupita said, opening the pantry door. But her mom closed it.

"The enchiladas con mole will be ready in an hour," Mama said. "No snacking before dinner."

Lupita's stomach cramped in protest.

"But I'm so hungry!" Lupita yelled, salivating at the thought of the rich mole sauce. "Please, just one small bag of Takis."

"Junk food?" Mama said. "Absolutely not. You know you need to watch your weight."

Lupita was too embarrassed to tell her mom about Nilda stealing her lunch money. So, on top of having just a tiny taquito for lunch, she had to miss out on snacking too. It wasn't fair.

Heat rose all the way from Lupita's jammed toe up through her belly into her face. Her eyes burned.

Lupita stared at the pot. The delicious smell curled through her nose and tickled her hunger.

She wanted to scream, but she swallowed it back. Anger built in her belly. Her eyes felt so hot they wanted to explode.

And then the heat was gone. Lupita's anger was calmed. And the flames under the pot of stew leapt up and caught the curtains.

"Ay Dios mio!" Mama exclaimed. She filled a pitcher and threw the water onto the curtain. Lupita grabbed the oven mitt and beat out the rest of the flames.

"You're not hurt, are you, mi hija?" Mama asked.

Lupita shook her head no. Her voice wouldn't come.

"What on earth happened?" Mama mumbled, checking the gas. The flames were at their normal, low burn.

Lupita left the kitchen, walking slowly on shaking legs. She sat at the living room table and looked out at the volcano.

Two times she may have caused fire. One, when she was frustrated at her math homework. The second, when she was angry that she couldn't have a snack.

Did the fire come from anger? Was she some kind of…fire witch?

Her eyes filled with hot tears, water after the fire. She put her head down and wove her fingers into her thick hair.

A creak made her look up. Abuela was watching her from her hammock.

"I'm OK," Lupita said and wiped her nose on her arm. "Just upset and confused."

Abuela usually wore the same, still expression in her face mapped with wrinkles. But Lupita swore the lines at her mouth turned down.

Abuela lifted a shaking hand and beckoned to Lupita. Lupita went over to the hammock. Abuela placed her surprisingly soft hands around one of Lupita's.

"Remember when we used to call this an Abuela hand-sandwich?" Lupita asked, studying her darker hand in between Abuela's tan ones.

She couldn't be sure, but she swore the wrinkles at Abuela's mouth turned up. It soothed her heart.

Lupita slipped her hand out and went to get her brother. The sooner they finished their homework, the sooner she could finally eat.

Chapter
Four

Lupita pulled the knitted blanket up to her chin. Though it was a warm night, she liked the comfort of the soft, thin material over her body. Her stomach was full of tasty enchiladas with spicy, chocolatey mole sauce. She couldn't even remember being hungry. She was too content.

Sleep took her quickly, and she fell into a dream.

The volcano stood under a star-filled sky. A line of people holding torches climbed the long path to the top. The people looked just like they did in the old family photo.

The women wore long dresses with full, ankle-length skirts. The men wore billowing shirts over trousers.

Lupita was floating above the volcano. Someone held her hand. It was Abuela.

Abuela pointed, and suddenly they were standing at the crater, close to the people at the front of the line.

The sound of drumming echoed in the night. At the crater, a woman in a long dress and dark shawl held the hand of a little girl. They were just like the woman and girl in the photo.

The woman turned her head and Lupita gasped.

It was true what Abuela always said. Lupita looked just like great-great-grandmother Nayeli.

Lupita felt a tug on her hand. Abuela pointed to the little girl. Then pointed to herself.

"That little girl is you?" Lupita asked.

Abuela nodded.

Lupita and the old Abuela stood at the rim of the volcano. Nayeli and the young Abuela also stood at the rim. Both Abuelas wore two long braids, though the old Abuela's braids were white, not dark.

Nayeli raised her hands and said some strange

words that didn't sound like Spanish. They must be Náhuatl, the language of Lupita's ancestors.

Nayeli carefully lay a red flower and an ear of corn by the volcano's crater. She helped the little girl do the same.

Then, in Spanish, Nayeli told the people that the volcano was calm and happy. They should always honor it with flowers and corn to keep it this way.

"That's beautiful," Lupita whispered aloud.

The old Abuela next to her smiled, showing her three remaining teeth. Then Abuela turned Lupita's wrist to show a dark red flower in Lupita's hand.

The drumming faded and Lupita blinked her eyes open in her quiet room. The curtain stirred in the breeze, and the half-moon lit everything in a soft silver blue. There was no sign of Abuela.

Lupita opened her hand. There was nothing in it.

Was it just a dream? Or had Abuela come to her and showed her the past?

Lupita turned in bed and gazed out the window at the volcano's sloping form. The slope was lit with silver from the hanging moon. No smoke disturbed the stars.

Lupita's ancestors used to honor the volcano with flowers and corn. Who honored it now?

Lupita felt a little sad for the volcano. But she couldn't do anything about it. Could she?

The thought kept her awake for the rest of the night.

Chapter
Five

Friday. It was supposed to be a good day. After all, school was over for the week. But today was terrible.

Lupita had not eaten any lunch. When Nilda stood over her at the end of history class, Lupita shook with a clammy fear. She lost her lunch money as usual. Carlos was at home with a cold, so there was no one to share food with her.

Weak and hungry. What a way to start the weekend.

With two tired arms, she pulled the front door to her house open. Her backpack dropped like a stone by the door.

The house was quiet. Abuela was asleep in the hammock. There were no sounds of Bernardo kicking a ball, no Mama and Papa talking in the kitchen.

Lupita felt her spirits lift. No Mama in the kitchen…that meant…

After two bags of Takis and a liter of agua de jamaica, iced hibiscus tea, Lupita felt energy run through her. She skipped into the living room, and her now clear eyes saw a note on the table.

Dear Lupita,

Papa and I are at Antonio's house. Come eat dinner with us. Or, reheat the pozole that is in the refrigerator and eat with Abuela. Your brother is having a sleepover at Raul's.

A big kiss,
Mama.

After the Takis, Lupita wasn't hungry anymore, not even for delicious stew. She could watch television, but Abuela was asleep. Lupita didn't want to disturb her.

She found herself going out the back door into the garden.

Lupita stopped and stared. On the ancient, spindly bush, a large flower the color of a royal pillow grew proudly. Lupita studied her open palm. She remembered the soft feel of the petals from her dream. Her mind replayed Nayeli and young Abuela laying the flowers by the crater.

Towering above the city, the volcano curled white smoke like a giant campfire.

Maybe there was a reason a flower grew on Nayeli's bush now. Lupita had held a red flower in her dream. Did it mean she should honor the volcano just as her ancestor Nayeli had done?

Lupita almost never rode the bicycle that sat rusting in their garage. Her parents brought it home last year. They thought Lupita needed more exercise. Carlos got one too. They went to the park and at first it went well. She actually enjoyed the rush of air as she sped ahead. Then she fell off and got all bruised.

With the bike, she could be at the volcano in about an hour.

Now that she had a mission, Lupita moved fast. She picked the velvety flower off the bush and put it in a bag. She wrote a quick note saying she went out for exercise and left it on the table. Then Lupita flew out of the house.

Lupita cycled the creaky bicycle on slanted sidewalks, past palm trees and colorful buildings. It was a bumpy ride, and she gripped the handles tight. Once she got to the edge of the city, she pumped her legs along the main road, which was smoother. Up and down rolling hills, past trees and scrub. There was plenty of shade and the road wasn't too busy. But the air was hot and dusty.

Before she knew it, Lupita was at the entrance to the trail going up the volcano.

Lupita couldn't wait for the rains to come next month. Sweat poured off her brow and her t-shirt was damp. She paused for a moment, took deep breaths and enjoyed the shade of the trees.

Slightly cooler but still sticky, she locked up the bicycle at the entrance to the path and started walking. The smell of fir trees refreshed the air and yellow flowers bloomed in clusters. But as she looked around, a heavy sadness filled her.

Though they often went to the ocean nearby, her family hadn't gone to the volcano for years. Now, Lupita's eyes filled with tears. The trail had changed.

Plastic bottles lined the sides of the path. A shiny package of Takis Fuego hung on the low branch of a tree. Waste was scattered as far as she could see up the path.

Lupita felt her feet drag as she climbed past soda cans and empty Bueno chocolate bar packages. She breathed hard. The bike ride had made her thighs heavy and exhausted. This steep climb felt too much.

But she kept going. She had come this far. The crater was getting closer.

Once she was up high, trees no longer grew. In front of her, a dry, sunny path stretched to the top.

Her town lay below her, the roofs of the houses

close together like an island in the tree-filled landscape. Green hills rolled in every direction but west. To the west, a sapphire blue ocean stretched out, refreshing and cool.

She took a branch to use as a walking stick. Though the trees were gone, the trash was gone too. At least not all of the volcano was covered with litter. It made her feel a little lighter.

Finally, she reached the top. She sat down heavily in the dry dirt. What was she thinking? Her legs were so tired. How would she get home?

The crater gave off a lot of heat, just a few steps away. Her stomach danced with nerves at the height and the power of the volcano she was actually on top of. What if it started shaking and blowing smoke again?

This was starting to feel like a crazy idea. She had better be quick.

The sun was angling low in the sky. It no longer burned and was a warm kiss on her skin. The walk up the volcano took longer than she expected. She must do what she came here to do before night fell.

Lupita pulled the now wilted red flower from her

bag. She came close to the crater. Her eyes stung from the heat.

She didn't know what her ancestor Nayeli would say. She wished she had better words but all she could think of was, "Here, volcano, a flower for you."

She lay it gently on the crater's edge, the memory of the litter along the path saddening her.

"I'm sorry," she said. With a deep sigh, she turned to go.

Chapter
Six

"Thank you," boomed a low voice.

Lupita tensed. She scanned the dusty mountain top, but saw no one.

She stared at the crater. Had the voice come from there? The smoke had stopped. Though there was warmth coming from the crater, it wasn't hot like before. She crept to the edge and peered in.

"Ay Dios mio!" Lupita said shakily. She was frozen to the spot in fear. Yellow flames filled the crater. It looked like two orange eyes watched her from the flames. Was she so exhausted that she was imagining things?

"Do not be afraid," the voice boomed again.

"Who...what are you?" Lupita asked.

"Do you promise not to be afraid?" came the loud answer.

"I don't think I can promise that," Lupita said, her knees shaking.

"I promise not to harm you," the low voice boomed from the crater.

"OK, I will try my best not to be scared," Lupita answered. She sank down to her knees. That way, she felt more stable. She placed her hands on the dry, warm ground for comfort.

A yellow semicircle rose out of the crater like a mini sun. Orange eyes appeared next, set in a face of flames. His head was as nearly as big as the crater.

"You're...a fire man," Lupita said, clutching her heart, which sped quickly ahead.

"I'm a fire giant," he said. "And no one has given me a flower in many turns of the sun."

The fire giant pulled his enormous, burning body up. He was as tall as a tree and man-shaped. Lupita craned her neck to look up at him.

Her heart sped up as the intense heat made her

sweat. Was she going to melt?

Then a curious thing happened. The fire giant shrank. He became almost human sized, but larger.

The giant sat at the lip of the crater. His flaming body was the same color as the yellow flowers in the woods. Lupita felt the heat of his fire-knees, which were pointed towards her. They watched each other from opposite sides of the crater.

"Why have the humans stopped bringing flowers to me?" the fire giant asked. She could feel his voice through her body like a drum.

"I think people just forgot," she answered with a shrug. When Nayeli died, the custom of bringing flowers stopped too. That's what Abuela said.

But why didn't Abuela keep the custom alive?

"I was sad when the flowers stopped," the fire giant said, curling a flaming fist. "But four seasons ago I became very angry about it."

"Four seasons. Spring, summer, fall, winter…you mean one year ago?" Lupita asked. The fire giant nodded, and yellow flames zipped into the sky.

"Why did you suddenly get angry?" Lupita asked. Even if she was imagining all this, it was interesting.

The fire giant swung his flaming legs back and forth as he sat. It didn't look like he was going to hurt her.

"I do not trust you enough to tell you," the fire giant said.

Lupita wound her fingers together as she thought. Could she get the fire giant to trust her?

"Did you know Nayeli Zocotan?" Lupita asked.

"Ah, Nayeli," the fire giant sighed. The flames around his heart grew a deep orange, the same color as his eyes. "She was the last of the fire worshippers. She was my friend. When she stopped visiting, I cried smoke tears."

"Well," Lupita said. "I'm her great-great-granddaughter, Lupita."

The fire giant stared at her like a cat. Lupita swallowed hard.

"I see her in you," the fire giant said. "She had the power of fire. Do you?"

Lupita's mouth fell open. Excitement zipped through her. Nayeli had…fire power?

Lupita thought back to her math homework burning, and the flames on the stove leaping high, catching the curtains. Now was a chance to tell someone…or something…about the strange fire in her.

Then she thought about Nilda taking her lunch money and how it made her feel shaky and damp.

"I think I do have fire power," Lupita said, brightening. "But I don't know how to use it."

The fire giant studied her. She found herself blinking under his hot stare.

"Come again, and I will teach you," he said.

Lupita felt more zips run through her.

"I'll come tomorrow, if I can get away," Lupita said. "It's Saturday, we don't have school."

A cry like a bird's call came from the crater. The flames around the fire giant's heart turned deep orange. The cries came again. What else was in the volcano?

"Is it a bird?" Lupita asked. She peered below her feet but the crater was dark.

The fire giant made a clucking noise. The cries fell silent.

"I have said many things today," the fire giant stated. "That is enough human talk for now."

There was so much Lupita wanted to know. What else was in the volcano? How could she control her fire power? But she would have to wait.

"I need to go anyway," Lupita said. "It will be hard to find my way in the dark."

Purple and pink streaks followed the sun, which had already set into the ocean.

Could she find her way in the dark? The road back to city wasn't well-lit.

Her legs felt like lead. She was too tired to cycle all the way home, especially in the dark. But she had to.

The fire giant darted his orange eyes around.

"Pick up that stick," he said, pointing a fiery finger at Lupita's walking stick.

Lupita held it out with both hands. The fire giant sent a spark from his finger, which landed on the end of the branch.

"A torch, to guide your way home," the fire giant said.

"Thank you," Lupita said, holding the flaming stick up. It was heavy, but she needed the light to see the path.

"It is I who thank you for the flower," the fire giant replied with a bow of his bright head.

Lupita bowed back, because she didn't know how to curtsy. She made her way down the path. At least in the dark evening, with just the small circle of light from the torch, she couldn't see the trash.

But she knew it was there.

Chapter
Seven

The weekend flew by. There was no time to visit the volcano. Lupita felt frustrated. She wanted the fire giant to teach her how to use her fire power.

But Saturday was her cousin's quinceañera, her fifteenth birthday, and there was a huge party. Lupita enjoyed a lot of food and didn't light anything on fire by accident, at least. And Sunday they took a family outing to the city to do some shopping for summer clothes. Lupita and Bernardo were 'growing too fast', her parents said. They couldn't wear last year's stuff.

Lupita was glad to have more room in her

sneakers. But she wished there had been time to visit the fire giant.

Monday morning, Lupita sighed as her history teacher talked about the volcano. She would much rather be at the volcano than staring at a picture of it.

Then Mr. Gonzalez said something that made her ears perk up.

"Our people had more respect for the volcano back then," he said. "In the past, we offered the volcano flowers. Some say the volcano is angry that we have forgotten it."

Was Mr. Gonzalez talking about the volcano being alive? Or did he know about the fire giant?

When class ended, Nilda started to come over as always. But Lupita was too interested in talking to Mr. Gonzalez to care about Nilda. Lupita grabbed her backpack and hurried over to him.

"Sir…" she said to her teacher's back as he was walking to the door.

"Lupita," Mr. Gonzalez said, turning. "Can I help you with something?"

"I think we should respect the volcano, like in

the past." Lupita chewed her lip. What if he didn't know about the fire giant? Then he would think she was making things up. So maybe she couldn't talk about him.

"Respect is very important," Mr. Gonzalez replied with a nod. "If we respect our environment, we take care of it."

"The litter!" Lupita said, the words racing out of her mouth before she could stop them. "I went to the volcano Friday. There were soda and beer cans along the path, everywhere!"

"That's shocking, Lupita," he said, scowling. "I haven't been to the volcano in years. How awful to hear that."

"Well, can we do something about it?" Lupita asked, surprising herself. A blaze inside her gave power to her words.

Mr. Gonzalez raised an eyebrow.

"How about a class cleanup?" he asked. "We'll clean up the path together, maybe have a picnic after."

"It would show the volcano we cared," Lupita said.

"I can tell you were listening to my lesson," he replied with a smile. "I'll arrange the class cleanup."

"Wow," Lupita said, feeling a tingle of happiness. The thought of the path actually being cleared of trash made her feel bright. She was glad she had shared her feelings with her teacher.

"Now, I need to go to lunch," Mr. Gonzalez said, taking a few steps to the door, briefcase in hand. Lupita wished she could walk out with him. But her history book was sitting on her desk.

She couldn't make her feet move back to her desk…and Nilda.

Lupita glanced at Carlos, who stood near the serape blanket on the wall. Carlos looked sad. Nilda's arms were crossed and she stared at Lupita with one eyebrow arched. A challenge.

Near the door, Mr. Gonzalez stopped by Carlos. He looked at him, then Nilda, then Lupita.

"A friend of yours?" he asked Lupita, meeting her eyes.

"Carlos is," she mumbled, heat building in her cheeks. Her throat was tight and she couldn't say anymore. She looked down, embarrassed.

"Lupita, how about I walk you to lunch?" Mr. Gonzalez spoke in a suddenly gentle voice. "I'm going to the canteen too."

"That would be great," Lupita said, relief washing through her. "Carlos, Mr. Gonzalez is walking us to the canteen." She said it loudly so Nilda would know she couldn't try anything.

Carlos shot a smile at her and gave her a thumbs-up.

Lupita grabbed her history book from under Nilda's nose and shoved it in her backpack. She walked out with Mr. Gonzalez and Carlos. Her steps felt light and easy.

For the first time in forever, Lupita paid for a hot lunch. She carried a tray of quesadillas to the table and gave Carlos her flan.

"For all the food you shared with me," Lupita said.

"You didn't have to," Carlos replied.

"OK, if you don't want it …" Lupita joked, taking it back. Carlos frowned until Lupita gave him the flan and lightly pinched him. They both giggled.

He ate the flan before his tacos.

"I can almost hear my stomach saying, 'hot food, hot food, thank you,'" Lupita said as she bit into a quesadilla.

"My stomach is saying, 'flan is all I ever need,'" Carlos joked, licking the spoon.

Lupita was so happy that when she noticed Nilda sitting alone, she quickly looked away. Because Nilda was holding her stomach without any lunch in front of her.

She didn't want to care. But she knew exactly how it felt to stare at an empty table, the smell of food all around. And she wouldn't wish it on anyone.

Chapter
Eight

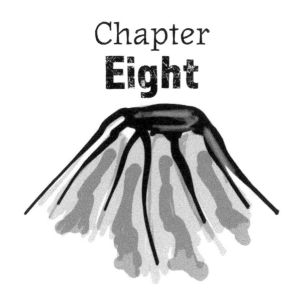

The next day, Lupita was happy. She tapped her pencil to a beat in her head as Mr. Gonzalez outlined the class trip to clear trash from the volcano's path.

"Lupita, please explain the problem to the class," Mr. Gonzalez said.

Lupita's pencil clattered to the floor. Everyone was looking at her. Nilda sneered.

Lupita's face was hot with embarrassment. She met Carlos' eye. He made an OK sign with his fingers and gave her a supportive nod.

"Well, there are beer cans and soda cans in the bushes," she explained in a weak voice. She cleared her throat, sounding like a car that wouldn't start. Her cheeks burned and she wished she could disappear.

"I saw that too," said Ana, a girl with long braids like Abuela's. "We went to the volcano last weekend. It was terrible." Ana nodded at Lupita, who felt a little stronger.

"There was a snack bag on a tree, waving like a flag," Lupita explained, her voice clearer.

Nilda rolled her eyes. Lupita tried not to notice.

"It's not fair that people litter," a boy near Carlos spoke up. "I jumped down from a tree in the park and slipped on a plastic bottle!" He showed the class his elbow, which was bruised.

"Exactly," Lupita said, feeling strength straighten her back. "Litter is not fair to us. It's not fair to the trees and it's not fair to the volcano."

Carlos gave her a thumbs-up.

"Thank you," Mr. Gonzalez said, winking at Lupita. "Next week on Monday we will take a bus to the volcano. Please have your parents sign a permission slip."

He handed them out and Lupita felt a thrill when

she noticed the time. Five minutes to lunch.

She fully expected Mr. Gonzalez to walk with her to the canteen again. Maybe they would speak more about the volcano. Maybe Lupita would tell him about the fire giant. She wondered what the hot food choices were today…

The next thing she knew, students were rushing out of the classroom. Mr. Gonzalez walked out the door, speaking on his cell phone.

Oh no…

Nilda strode over to Lupita's desk.

Lupita waited for the usual clammy hands and shaky weakness in her body. But it didn't happen. Why wasn't she afraid?

A picture of Nilda sitting alone in the canteen without lunch swam into her mind.

Nilda crossed her arms and loomed over Lupita. But Lupita wasn't scared. She felt sorry for Nilda. Surprised at her strength and steadiness, she stood up.

"Look, Nilda, I'm sorry you have no lunch money," Lupita said, crossing her arms too. "But it's not fair to take mine."

Nilda blinked up at her. Because after all, Lupita was taller. After a tense few seconds, Nilda spoke.

"I guess you've done enough," Nilda said. "It's time for me to train someone else to pay for lunch."

Lupita felt a wave of relief. Was it really all over? No more Nilda bullying?

But it was too soon to be relaxed. Lupita's shoulders tensed all the way to her ears as Nilda strode towards Carlos. Her best friend, shaking, backed up into the corner.

"Hey!" Lupita shouted, heat running through her body from her feet to her scalp.

"Changed your mind?" Nilda asked, holding out her hand, palm up.

Lupita opened her mouth to tell Nilda to leave Carlos alone. But the heat was faster. It built in her stomach and rushed out her mouth. The ends of Nilda's hair caught fire. Nilda shrieked.

"Ay Dios mio!" Carlos yelled. He ripped the serape blanket off the wall and patted Nilda's hair with it.

The fire was soon out. Smoke curled from the ends of Nilda's hair. Carlos took a big step away from Nilda, who was shaking where she stood.

"Are you...are you burned?" Lupita asked, wringing her hands.

Nilda swayed.

"Fire came out of your mouth," Nilda said, backing up towards the door. "What's wrong with you?" Her hands were up, as if warding off Lupita. When she got to the door, she turned and ran out of the room.

"Carlos, you were so quick, that was amazing," Lupita gushed with relief. The fire was out, Nilda was gone, no one got hurt. Everything was OK.

Except that Carlos didn't answer.

He just stared at Lupita like Nilda had, eyes wide and hands shaking with fear.

Chapter
Nine

Carlos hurried out of the classroom before Lupita could stop him. Her throat felt raw and warm. The fire had escaped her without warning. And now Carlos, her best friend, was afraid of her.

Even though she had her lunch money, Lupita had lost her appetite. She wasn't sure Carlos would want to sit with her today. The thought of eating all alone made her feel sick.

She still had three classes after lunch. But she needed to leave now. The fire giant was the only one who could help her.

So she walked. Her feet pounded the paved

streets of the city. She walked through the park, under palm trees. She passed through the white arches of an old mansion. She was so upset that the normally mouth-watering, sugary scents from the churro stand made her feel sick.

She left the city and kept walking down the road. *Pound, pound, pound* went her feet across rolling hills of scrub. She finally reached the bottom of the volcano.

It must have taken hours to walk here. Her legs were weak and tired. But she slowly climbed the trash-lined path. When she got to the top of the crater, she sank to her knees and cried.

A blast of heat covered her body. A fiery head of yellow flames filled the crater. The fire giant swung an enormous arm onto the dirt. He pulled himself up, a huge, flaming creature bigger than the cathedral itself.

Lupita felt intense heat all over her skin. She covered her face with her arm. The fire giant shrank, his flames burning lower. He sat, a giant man of flames, on the other side of the crater.

"What's wrong?" the fire giant asked in his low

voice.

"Well," she sniffed. "I set fire to Nilda's hair and now Carlos is afraid of me." Her words rushed out.

"Is Carlos your friend?" the fire giant asked.

Lupita nodded.

"If he is your friend he will understand," the fire giant boomed.

"Maybe I'm afraid too," Lupita said. "I don't know how it happened. The fire just…shot out."

"Did you feel angry?" the fire giant asked.

"Very," Lupita said, imagining Nilda striding towards poor Carlos. Her best friend stood shaking in the corner. It wasn't fair.

"Anger is not something to be afraid of," the fire giant said.

"But I could have hurt Nilda," Lupita said. "I didn't mean to set fire to her hair."

The fire giant nodded, flames licking into the sky as he moved his head.

"We can feel angry and not set anything on fire," he explained.

"How can I do that?" Lupita asked.

"It's not so hard," the fire giant said.

Lupita's mind was racing through memories of Nilda's hair on fire, Carlos' fearful stare and the trash lining the path.

"I'm so angry now," Lupita said, feeling the heat build inside her.

"Deep breaths," the fire giant said. "Think of the ocean or something good."

"Does that work?" Lupita asked.

"I do it all the time," the fire giant said. "Practice every night before you sleep. Then, in time, you will be able to control your fire power."

Lupita wasn't sure. Her anger was intense, the fire powerful.

"I started a whole forest fire by accident once," the fire giant confessed. "I learned to control my power. You can too."

A whole forest fire?

Lupita studied the yellow giant swinging his legs on the crater. He seemed calm, though he was made of fire.

Lupita felt a little hope. The tightness in her belly relaxed. Maybe she could learn not to light fires with her anger.

"I have good news for you," Lupita said. She told the fire giant about the path clean-up.

The fire giant's eyes widened.

"That is good news," he said. "I thought the humans didn't care about the land."

"We do care," Lupita said. "Many of us love this volcano, the path, the trees and everything."

The fire giant nodded.

"Then it's time," he said.

"For what?" Lupita asked.

"I will share my secret with you," he said. To Lupita's surprise, he peered into the crater and cooed.

Chapter
Ten

Lupita's palms sweat when a head of golden flames poked out of the crater.

The head had a shimmering yellow beak. Its orange eye met Lupita's gaze.

The fire giant made clucking sounds.

A huge, golden bird made of fire lifted out of the crater. It soared through the sky like a comet, then came down to land next to the fire giant. Its tail was longer than a peacock's, twisting gold and yellow flames. It trained a wide eye on Lupita.

"This is my son," the fire giant said.

Questions crowded her mind. Did they live

together in the volcano? How old was his son?

The question that came out of her mouth was, "Why is he a bird?"

The fire giant stroked the bird's flaming head. Their flames matched – yellow-gold. Except the fire giant had orange flames around his heart.

His heart flames had turned orange when he talked about Nayeli. Maybe when he felt love, that's what happened.

"Young fire giants can take many forms," the fire giant explained. "Sometimes Queple is a fox, sometimes a shooting star. His favorite form is this one, a bird."

Queple tilted his head and squawked, sending sparks up into the sky.

"OK," Lupita said, wringing her hands and trying to understand. "So…is there a Mama?"

The fire giant looked out west, towards the ocean. The water was already touched with the first pink of sunset. The fire giant sighed and all his flames turned orange.

"His Mama, the most beautiful Fiera, lives deep under the ocean in a volcano," he said. "I used to visit her all the time. Now, I need to stay and watch over Queple. So I cannot go."

"That's sad," Lupita said. "So you haven't seen her in a long time?"

"Four seasons ago, Queple was born under the ocean," the fire giant explained. He bowed his head and tiny flames licked into the air as he spoke. "It is too dangerous for a young one to live under all that water.

I covered myself with earth and shot through the ocean. I carried him close, so he was surrounded by fire. I haven't seen Fiera since then."

The fire giant gazed out to sea again, his orange flames matching the sunset.

"I'm sorry," Lupita said. It sounded so sad. The fire giant hadn't seen his love for a year. And Queple and his Mama hadn't seen each other either.

Lupita's heart softened. She wanted to help.

"Can Fiera come live with you?" she asked.

"Fiera will never leave her home," the fire giant said, shaking his head. "She loves it under the ocean. All her friends are there."

Lupita wondered what creatures were the friends of an underwater fire giant. Octopuses? Mermaids? Sharks? She shivered.

The fire giant sparked yellow jets of flame into the sky.

"One day I will live with her under the water," he said. "But it is not safe for Queple here, all alone.

I worry what people will do if they discover him." He met Lupita's eye with his blazing eyes.

Lupita felt a shudder through her body. She wanted to tell him Queple was safe. But images of the beautiful, fiery bird behind bars in a zoo flashed in front of her.

She couldn't promise that people wouldn't hurt him.

People littered. They trapped animals in zoos. Not everyone was good.

Lupita looked at her hands.

"Are you angry at people?" Lupita asked, meeting the fire giant's eyes again.

"Very," he said. "And if I didn't breathe deep and think of the ocean, I would have erupted the volcano by now."

Images of lava snaking towards the city filled her mind. Sounds of people screaming and visions of people running were in her head. Fear clenched her heart.

"Please don't erupt," she pleaded.

The fire giant stared.

"I don't want to hurt you," he said.

The sun dipped into the ocean, leaving a trail of ember orange and lava red across the sky and the water.

Another thought gripped Lupita's heart with fear.

"It's night!" Lupita said. "Oh no, I'm going to get in so much trouble."

"You are supposed to be home?" the fire giant asked.

"Yes, and it will take hours to walk home," Lupita pulled at her hair. "I'll be yelled at and even grounded!"

"We can get you home quickly," the fire giant said. "But you must trust me."

Lupita's eyes grew wide as the fire giant made clicking noises to Queple. She hoped he wouldn't ask her to ride a flaming bird. She'd get burned.

Queple flew down the mountain. He came back with an enormous branch in his golden claw. Lupita tensed. It was way too big for her to carry. The fire giant murmured over it. Fire shot out the back end of the branch.

"Ride this home," he said.

"Um…is that safe?" Lupita said nervously as the branch floated towards her, like a witch's broom.

"You will be fine," he said. "Unless you want to walk?"

There was a small chance her parents wouldn't be home yet. If she walked, she would get in trouble for sure.

Lupita carefully climbed onto the branch, scooting forward from the fiery back. Her heart pounded. She was actually going to ride a magic branch!

"Sit in the center for balance," the fire giant explained. "The flames won't burn you, they move away from the end of the broom. Like a comet."

"OK," Lupita said nervously. She shifted backwards until the fire giant made a flaming OK sign with his fingers.

"Now tell it where you want to go," the fire giant said.

"Home," Lupita said.

The flaming branch made a mighty lurch and shot into the sky. Lupita's stomach turned over and she grabbed the wood tight. Her eyes shut as the cool, night air whooshed over her.

She peeked open an eyelid and saw the tiny lights of the city below. Her head spun, not just with the height. She was actually on a magic branch, flying through the night. Wonder and awe made her smile. Magic was real, really real. And she could fly!

Excitement tingled through her body, and she let out a whoop!

The wind on her face lessened. The branch was slowing. She was carried past the roof of her house into the garden.

Her feet touched the ground and she gratefully climbed off. She grinned and wished Carlos was here so she could tell him – show him – she could fly.

The branch hovered, the end smoking.

"Thank you?" she asked the branch, not sure what to say. It soared back up into the sky. It went high, and as it moved towards the volcano, it looked like a shooting star.

Lupita's smile disappeared when she passed the kitchen window to go into the house. A face at the window stared out at her. Someone had seen her.

Abuela.

Chapter
Eleven

Lupita's hand shook as she turned the knob of the front door. She could be in big trouble if her parents were home. But was she in bigger trouble with Abuela?

Lupita had landed in the garden on a flying branch. What if Abuela was frightened, like Nilda and Carlos? She couldn't handle Abuela being afraid of her.

Lupita entered the house. It was quiet and dark, except for a glow coming from the kitchen. She flipped on the living room light.

Smells of cilantro and peppers made her

stomach rumble. But she couldn't think about eating now. Abuela stood at the archway to the kitchen, her dark eyes fixed on Lupita's.

Lupita felt her shoulders sag. She didn't want to be scary. She bowed so low she nearly crawled to Abuela.

"Sorry I'm late," Lupita said, looking up. "And sorry about…how I got here."

Abuela opened her hand and gestured to the table. Lupita saw there was a note. She sank down on a wooden chair. Her legs were so tired from the long walk to the volcano.

"So they are all out again," Lupita said, reading the note. What luck. If Abuela didn't tell her parents she got home so late, they would never know. But would Abuela tell them about the ride on the flaming branch?

Abuela shuffled out of the kitchen holding a hot bowl of something steaming. She placed it in front of Lupita, next to a plate full of tortillas.

Lupita took a deep sniff of corn and tangy chili peppers. Plus, there was something extra. A secret ingredient Lupita couldn't guess. This wasn't just any stew.

"You cooked!" Lupita said with a smile, forgetting all her worries.

Abuela didn't seem angry or scared at all. Maybe Abuela hadn't seen her land in the garden. It was dark outside after all.

Lupita ate a spoonful, tasting the wonderful blend of herbs. Joy warmed her, right down to her toes.

This was Abuela's special stew. The one Mama tried to make but just couldn't get right. Abuela almost never cooked anymore.

"Does this mean you were feeling strong today?" Lupita asked Abuela, who sat with a cup of mint tea.

Abuela's dark eyes gleamed and the hint of a smile danced at the corners of her mouth. She squeezed Lupita's shoulder and shuffled down the hallway that led to her room. Maybe she was going to bed. Lupita hoped she wasn't too tired from cooking.

Lupita forgot any worries as she rolled up a corn tortilla and dipped it into the stew. She ate so fast that she barely breathed.

When she finished, she sat back, satisfied. She felt sleepy and held her full stomach.

Outside the window, the volcano stood, silvery in the moonlight. Lupita wondered what fire giants ate. Probably not Abuela's best stew.

The sound of slippers on hardwood made Lupita perk up. Abuela shuffled back into the room with a woven wrap around her shoulders. She was holding something.

An envelope, yellow with age. Abuela pulled out an old photo and lay it on the table. Surprise woke Lupita up completely.

A woman who looked just liked Lupita held out her hand, palm up. In the old photo, a glowing ball hovered just over her hand.

Chapter
Twelve

Lupita examined the black and white photograph with quiet amazement. The glowing ball seemed to hover over the woman's palm. The woman looked a lot like her, except so calm and peaceful.

"Abuela," Lupita asked, "Is this Nayeli with…a fireball?"

Abuela tapped her wrinkled finger on the woman in the photograph, then tapped Lupita's shoulder. A tingling excitement rushed through Lupita's body. Abuela knew about fire power! Nayeli had it, just as the fire giant had said.

Lupita had a tumble of questions and turned to

ask them but stopped.

Abuela's eyes were half closed. Her wrinkled hand gripped the chair back and she slumped heavily.

"Oh no, after cooking you must be so tired," Lupita said, her excitement damped down with worry.

Lupita slung her great-grandmother's shoulder over hers and wrapped an arm around her bony, fragile waist. Abuela smelled of cilantro, chili and talcum powder.

Lupita helped her shuffle to her room down the hall. Lupita almost never came in here. It smelled heavily of powder and jasmine, the flowery scent coming in through the open window.

She helped her great-grandmother into bed, pulling the sheet and striped serape blanket over her.

"Want me to tell you a bedtime story?" Lupita whispered.

Though Abuela's eyes were already closed, a smile broke through the wrinkles at the corners of her mouth.

"Once upon a time there was a young girl who loved sweet, coconut empanadas," Lupita began. "She was eating one, enjoying the burst of coconut and brown sugar on her tongue, when a man walked by. He smiled..."

Lupita told the story of how Abuela met her husband. Abuela's smile deepened as Lupita continued the story of Abuela's first love, long ago. No one knew how long, maybe not even Abuela. Maybe a century?

When Lupita got to the part about the runaway donkey, Abuela started to snore. Lupita tiptoed out of the room. She sat by her empty bowl and studied the photo. Questions crowded her mind.

If Nayeli could control a fireball so it hovered over her hand, could Lupita? Who knew about Nayeli's fire power? Why had Abuela kept this photo hidden?

Lupita sighed with frustration. The volcano stood peaceful outside the window, smokeless under the stars and crescent moon. She wondered if Queple and the fire giant slept too.

Lupita needed answers. Abuela was usually

the first one awake. If Lupita could get out of bed in time, she could ask her questions then. Maybe Abuela would even feel strong enough to write down some answers for her.

The plan formed, Lupita decided to go to sleep early tonight. Of course, not before eating another big bowl of Abuela's best stew.

As she licked the bowl clean, she felt a heavy ache in her heart. It had been so long since Abuela last cooked. Who knew when her grandmother would find the strength to cook again?

The next morning, Lupita woke up at dawn to the ringing of her alarm. She tucked the photo into her skirt pocket. As she skipped down the stairs, she hoped Abuela would be strong enough to communicate with her.

Dawn had only just begun. The birds were chirping as they loudly greeted the sun. Abuela was already resting in her hammock in the living room. Her dark eyes met Lupita's.

Lupita opened her mouth to ask her about the photo, when an unexpected voice came from the kitchen.

"How was your night, mi hija?" Lupita's mom appeared, wearing her apron.

"Mama?" Lupita asked. "Isn't it like, ridiculously early?"

"I'm often up at this time," she said. "And why are you awake?" Her mom's eyes narrowed as if Lupita was acting suspicious.

"Oh just, I don't know, couldn't sleep." Lupita stretched and yawned to act relaxed.

"I felt bad leaving you and Abuela alone again last night, so I'm making scrambled eggs this morning," she said.

"With nopales?" Lupita asked, hopefully. She loved the tasty cactus pieces in scrambled eggs. It was the best breakfast.

"Of course!" Mama replied with a grin.

"Great! Thanks, Mama," Lupita said with real happiness.

"Honey, wake our son!" Lupita's mom yelled up the stairs to Papa before popping back into the kitchen. There was some stomping and a muffled 'no' as her brother begged for more sleep.

Lupita sat at the table to wait. She couldn't ask

Abuela about Nayeli and the fireball with her mom around. But it was OK if she was getting nopalitos con huevo.

A knock at the door added to the noisy morning.

"See who that is, Lupita," her mom yelled from the kitchen.

Maybe it was an early delivery from the mailman? When she opened the door, though, she stopped still with surprise.

Carlos stood there holding a bag of sugar. He looked at her with huge eyes and beads of sweat on his brow. Lupita bit her lip. Yesterday fire had come out of her mouth and burned Nilda's hair. It must have been scary for Carlos to see that.

But she didn't want Carlos to be afraid.

How could she get her best friend back?

Chapter
Thirteen

"Good morning, Carlos," Lupita said softly, hoping to calm him down. His right foot stepped behind his left like a nervous deer. Was he about to run?

The door was pulled out of Lupita's grasp and swung all the way open. Lupita turned to see Mama, who had just opened the door wide.

"Carlos!" Mama said. "Your mother told me you were returning the sugar I lent."

"Good morning, Mrs. Cuevas," Carlos said. He thrust a package into Mama's hands.

"What a helpful boy." Mama took his thin arm and led him into the house. "It has been so long.

When did we last see you?"

"Um," Carlos muttered, scanning the room, "Lupita's birthday party, I think."

"Well, I am happy you are here," her mom said. "You are just in time for eggs."

Carlos stood in the middle of the living room, wringing his hands.

"Just stay here with Lupita and they'll be ready in a minute," her mom said, dancing into the kitchen with the bag of sugar.

"Oh, could I help?" Carlos said, scurrying after her.

Lupita felt a deep weight on her shoulders. Her best friend hated cooking. He was definitely afraid to be with her.

She glanced at Abuela, hoping to share her sadness through just a look. Abuela would understand. But she was sleeping.

Lupita slumped into the chair at the kitchen table. Bernardo came down the stairs and raced into the living room, ready for breakfast. Papa came down more slowly and soon everyone but Abuela was sitting at the table.

Carlos sat between Bernardo and Papa, instead of next to her.

Lupita's mom placed a scoop of eggs on each plate. Lupita grabbed a warmed tortilla. The tasty egg-and-tortilla combo did a lot to lessen Lupita's sadness.

By the end of the meal, Carlos was smiling and laughing with the family. But he never looked at Lupita once.

She knew he was totally freaked out with the whole setting-Nilda's-hair-on-fire incident. There was no way she could tell him about her flight on the flaming branch. Sadness slumped her shoulders. She glanced at her sleeping grandmother. There was no one she could talk to anymore.

It was time to go to school. They strapped their backpacks on and stepped out the door. Would Carlos run away?

As soon as Mama shut the door with a goodbye, Carlos turned to her.

"What happened?" Carlos asked with steady eyes.

She raised an eyebrow.

"You know what I'm talking about," he said, crossing his arms in a very unlike–Carlos way.

No words came to her. How could she possibly explain?

So she pulled out the black and white photograph from her pocket. Her great-great-grandmother held out her palm and a glowing ball hovered over it. He studied it, his hand shaking.

"So it's real this…fire power," he asked, looking up.

"Yes, but it was an accident," Lupita said, hoping he would believe her. "I really didn't mean to set Nilda's hair on fire!"

"You could have really hurt her," Carlos said.

"I know," Lupita said, breakfast suddenly feeling heavy in her stomach. "You have to believe me. It wasn't on purpose."

"So you can't control the fire power?" Carlos asked.

Lupita shook her head.

"I wish you had told me about it," Carlos said, arms still crossed.

"I didn't know how to," Lupita said. "Ask me

anything, I'll tell you now."

Carlos studied her.

"Who is this?" he asked her, holding up the photo.

"My great-great-grandmother, Nayeli," Lupita replied.

"She looks like she is controlling her fire power," Carlos said, meeting Lupita's eyes.

In the photo, Nayeli had a smile on her face as the ball of fire hovered over her palm.

"Well, I can't," Lupita said. "Not yet. Though there is someone who can teach me to control it."

"Who?" Carlos asked, cocking an eyebrow.

"I can't explain…you would never believe me," Lupita said. "But I can show you. Tomorrow, after school?"

Carlos gazed at her like a cat. Lupita swallowed. The silent stare was nerve-wracking.

"Not sure I trust you," he said.

"How can you not trust me? I'm your best friend. Please, I really need to show you," Lupita babbled, her voice getting faster and higher. "No one else knows, and you can help me."

"OK," Carlos said. He shifted on his feet.

"We will need our bikes," Lupita said. "We'll go from school tomorrow."

"Yuck! I hate bikes," Carlos said. "You know that."

"We need to go to the volcano," Lupita explained. "Bikes are the fastest way to get there."

To her relief, Carlos nodded. They walked to school in silence, which felt painful.

At least Carlos had agreed to come with her tomorrow. The fire giant would be able to explain everything, Lupita felt sure of it.

And then maybe she'd have her best friend back.

Chapter
Fourteen

The next day, Lupita had lunch alone. Carlos ate with a boy he sat next to in science class. His back was to Lupita, halfway across the noisy canteen.

Lupita sighed and bit into her sopes, enjoying the crispy corn base with spicy salsa on top. At least she had lunch. That was something. Nilda hadn't even looked at her after history class.

She finished the sopes and started on the smooth flan for dessert. Somehow, she couldn't enjoy it. The flan reminded her too much of Carlos.

Would he still come with her to the volcano after school? She shook him from her mind, her heart heavy.

Her class had a plan to clean up trash from the volcano's path on Monday. At least that had been something good Lupita had done.

Lupita hoped she was a good person. Not a scary fireball of anger, which is how Nilda and Carlos probably saw her.

Lupita daydreamed through her next classes. She thought about her great-great-grandmother Nayeli. How did she manage to look so calm and happy in the photo while creating a fireball? Who knew about her fire power? Who took the picture?

She daydreamed about last summer. She and Carlos had gone to the beach with their families. They had laughed so much, splashing each other in the surf. Things were easier back then. Abuela still talked lots, and she didn't have any of this crazy fire power.

Her heart in her throat, Lupita went straight to the back of the building after school. Her bike was parked against a tree. Another bike leaned nearby. Would Carlos show?

Phew. His small frame exited the school doors.

He walked towards her with his backpack slung on his shoulder. She prayed she could win him back.

"OK, this had better be good," Carlos said, unlocking his bike.

"It will explain a lot," Lupita promised. She was so relieved he showed up, she barely noticed Nilda listening nearby.

"Prepare for a big surprise," Lupita said with a smile as they cycled down the bumpy street. Carlos didn't smile back.

Chapter
Fifteen

Silently, Lupita and Carlos cycled the hot, dusty road to the volcano. Silently, they locked up their bikes at the base of the path. Lupita climbed, Carlos followed. Lupita swore she could feel his mistrusting stare on the back of her head.

"I can see what you mean about the trash," Carlos finally voiced. She glanced back as he took a Doritos package off a branch of a fir tree.

"Isn't it terrible?" Lupita said, her voice way too squeaky. She was so relieved he spoke to her, the words had rushed out.

They walked the rest of the way in silence. Lupita

hoped once Carlos met the fire giant, they could go back to normal. Carlos would understand that Lupita had to keep the fire giant secret. He was too unbelievable to explain.

When they got to the top, there was no smoke coming from the crater. No flaming giant, either. Not even a forehead.

"Fire giant!" Lupita called out, stepping near the crater. Heat rose from it like an oven. "Please, I want you to meet my best friend."

"What are you doing?" Carlos said, standing far back from the crater. He looked like he was going to run back down the path. Far away from her.

"I know it sounds crazy, but please wait," Lupita pleaded. The dark crater looked deep and mysterious. Her eyes watered from the heat as she peered in. "A fire giant lives here. It can help me control my fire power."

"If I hadn't seen flames coming from your mouth when you attacked Nilda, I wouldn't believe you at all," Carlos said from the path, his voice small. "Now, I don't know what to believe."

"I didn't mean to attack her," Lupita said, turning

to face him. "I just lost control."

But Carlos wasn't looking at her anymore. He was looking past her.

Lupita felt great heat on the back of her head and all down her body. She hurried away from the crater and stood by Carlos on the path's edge. The fire giant rose out of the volcano, his head of flames sparking. The heat was almost too painful to bear.

Thankfully, the heat lessened to gentle warmth as the fire giant shrank. He sat on the opposite side of the crater, a giant man made of yellow flames.

"Wha - what are you?" Carlos stuttered. He crouched down to the ground.

"Don't be afraid," Lupita told Carlos.

"Why do you bring another human here?" the fire giant asked in a deep, rumbling voice. Yellow flames shot from his head into the sunny sky.

"He's my best friend," Lupita explained.

"Is this true?" the fire giant asked. He fixed his burning, orange eyes on Carlos.

Carlos' mouth moved and seemed to say 'yes'.

"You can trust him," Lupita said, both to the fire giant and Carlos. "Don't be afraid of each other, please."

Carlos stood up, his knees knocking.

"Carlos never litters," Lupita told the fire giant. "He is excited about our class cleanup."

"You respect the land?" the fire giant asked Carlos.

"Of course," Carlos replied. He breathed hard.

"We can all be friends," Lupita said to the fire giant. She tried to smile big, hoping everyone would relax.

The fire giant didn't smile.

"You want me to be...friends with that thing?" Carlos whispered to Lupita.

"Please try," Lupita said, squeezing his hand. "My great-great-grandmother Nayeli was friends with the fire giant, just like me."

She pulled the photo out of her pocket, showing it to Carlos and then the fire giant.

"Can you teach me how to control the fire, like she could?" Lupita asked.

For the first time, she heard the fire giant laugh. It sounded like cracking wood mixed with bird song. The yellow flames around his heart turned orange.

"You already know how to control fire," the fire giant said.

Lupita thought back to her flaming math homework, the kitchen curtains on fire, and then Nilda's hair smoking.

"I can't control it," she said, shaking her head sadly.

"Make friends with fire," the fire giant explained.

"How do I do that?" Lupita asked.

"You are good at it," the fire giant replied. "Show it respect and warmth. Just as you made friends with me and Carlos."

It sounded so easy. Would it be?

Chapter
Sixteen

The fire giant had laughed. Carlos wasn't shaking anymore, and the fire giant's heart flames were orange. Maybe no one was scared, and they were all becoming friends. Lupita hoped so.

Then Lupita heard the voice.

"What is that horrible thing?" someone yelled from the path. Someone familiar.

It was Nilda. What was she doing here?

The fire giant glared from his seat on the crater. His heart flames changed back to yellow. He stood up.

"I am not a thing," the fire giant said, growing

larger. "I am a fire giant."

"I don't like monsters," Nilda said, staying back on the path.

"Is this another of your friends?" the fire giant asked Lupita. Flames licked in every direction. Lupita and Carlos had to join Nilda where she stood. The heat was too strong to be any closer - like the hottest oven.

Nilda crouched to hide behind Lupita.

"Nilda is not my friend," Lupita explained, shielding her eyes from the smoke the fire giant gave off. Her heart pounded angrily. How did Nilda get here? She must have followed them.

"She called me a horrible thing!" the fire giant roared. "I do not like that." He jumped into the crater, disappearing.

"Why did you follow us?" Lupita yelled at Nilda, wishing she would disappear. Nilda had ruined everything.

"I wish I hadn't," Nilda said, her voice high and sharp. "I knew you were hiding something. I just didn't realize how terrible it was."

"The fire giant isn't terrible," Lupita argued.

"It should be put out!" Nilda said. "I'll tell people and we'll bring lots of water."

"No, he doesn't want any trouble," Lupita pleaded. An image of the fire giant turning into a steam cloud made Lupita's whole body shake.

"Well, that's too bad," Nilda said. "Because monsters get trouble."

"He's not a monster!" Lupita yelled. "He's my friend!"

"Maybe that makes you a monster too," Nilda shouted back.

The heat in Lupita's belly wanted to escape, to burn. But Carlos would never forgive Lupita if she let the fire burn Nilda again.

So Lupita swallowed hard, and pushed the fire, with all her will, down. Her throat felt tight and her belly was uncomfortably hot. But at least her fire power was under control.

"Go ahead, Nilda," Lupita said with her arms crossed. "Tell everyone you saw a big, scary monster. See if they believe you."

Nilda dug into her bag and pulled out a soda can. "This is what I think of you and your fire giant!"

Nilda arced her hand back as if to throw the can. Carlos reached up and grabbed Nilda's arm. She easily tore her arm from his grasp and threw the soda can into the smoking crater.

Lupita was so surprised she let go of the fire, which raced up from her belly, through her body and out her mouth. The fireball shooting from Lupita's mouth didn't reach Nilda, who had run down the path. It fell in the dirt and fizzled out. Lupita was only partially sorry Nilda hadn't gotten burned.

Lupita touched her throat, which felt warm and open. She never would have guessed breathing fire would feel so good.

Carlos was staring at Lupita again.

"Sorry," Lupita said to Carlos, her voice coming out shaky. "I can't control the fire…yet."

"We have a bigger problem," Carlos said.

The fire giant had jumped out of the crater. He stood with one foot on each side of the crater, as big as a house. Yellow flames licked out in every direction. Lupita threw her arm up to shield her eyes from the heat.

"She is everything that is wrong with humans!" the fire giant yelled, his voice echoing.

"I didn't know she was following us, I swear," Lupita pleaded. "Is Queple OK?" She hoped the can didn't upset the beautiful fiery bird.

"Who's Queple?" Carlos asked but Lupita didn't answer. She was worried the fire giant might explode. He was as big as a parota tree.

"The can hit my son's head," the fire giant roared, sparks shooting out of his mouth. Lupita and Carlos squatted down, shielding their faces with their arms.

"Queple is not safe," the fire giant roared as he grew taller, a tower of yellow flames. "That girl threatened us with water!"

It was way too hot. Sweat rolled down Lupita's forehead and back of her neck.

"You must leave!" the fire giant roared. "I am flaming hotter and it is not safe for humans!"

"What can I do to fix this?" Lupita said, wringing her hands.

"Come on!" Carlos yelled and tugged on Lupita's arm, trying to pull her down the path.

"Go!" the giant's voice crashed like thunder. "I will flame through this whole night. I am so angry!" A spark shot out from the fire giant's head and scorched the earth near Lupita's foot.

She turned and tried to run down the path with Carlos. But Lupita's legs tangled and she fell to her knees. She choked back a sob. This was all her fault.

Sparks shot out of the volcano and the earth rumbled. When the shaking stopped, Carlos pulled her to her feet.

Then, they ran.

Chapter
Seventeen

Lupita and Carlos made it down the path and started cycling home. Her legs and whole body felt heavy. This was all her fault. She should have never brought her best friend here. And how had she missed Nilda following them?

With a sound like rumbling thunder, the earth shook. It turned Lupita's bike wheel this way and that. She clamped her hands down hard on the handlebars. Breathing fast, she struggled to keep the bike balanced.

A sudden jolt shook Lupita's hands off the handlebars completely. The wheel turned, she skidded to the side and the bike fell on top of her.

"Ouch!" Carlos yelled with a crashing noise. Lupita twisted around to see.

"Oh no, Carlos," she said. He had fallen too, and was holding his arm close to his chest. His jaw was clenched tight.

"It hurts!" he said through his teeth.

The earth was still rumbling. Lupita slowly lifted her bike. She was OK apart from a stinging, scraped knee. But was Carlos?

Another earthquake shook the ground. Carlos hadn't gotten up yet, so Lupita held her hand out to him. He took it with his left, keeping his right hand close to him like a broken wing.

"I hate that giant," he said, spitting the words through his teeth.

"The fire giant is angry because he's afraid for his son, Queple," Lupita said. "Nilda threw a can right into the crater."

"I can't believe you thought it was your friend," Carlos said.

"He is my friend," Lupita said.

"Some friend!" Carlos yelled. "That thing is

going to destroy our city."

"He wouldn't do that!" Lupita shouted. She hoped it was true. Her stomach twisted with worry.

"Look around you!" Carlos shouted. He winced and clutched his arm to his chest. Thick smoke billowed out of the volcano's top.

"So, the volcano always smokes," Lupita said.

"It's never that thick!" Carlos argued.

"Let's get home," Lupita said. Maybe by then the fire giant would calm down. There would be no smoke, no rumbling earth.

Carlos couldn't ride because of his hurt arm. They had to walk. Lupita pushed the bikes down the road, one in each hand.

The next earthquake kicked the wheels out from the bikes. They both fell over. A pedal banged into Lupita's shin.

Flames shot out the top of the crater, bright red against the blue sky.

"I should go back," Lupita said, breathless. "Talk to him."

"You'd die!" Carlos yelled. "It's a monster! You'd be burned up in…"

Then Carlos' words stopped. Lupita followed her friend's silent stare. A hot bloom of bright orange lava covered the top of the volcano. It slowly crept down the cone of the mountain.

"It's really erupting!" Carlos shrieked. "We need to get home."

Lupita gulped, a heavy feeling in her gut. How could the fire giant erupt the volcano? How could he do this to her?

Lupita's house was closest, though it felt like forever before they got there. The sky was already twilight blue. A thick column of smoke blocked the sunset to the west.

She could see their house down the road, their car outside. Mama was throwing suitcases into the trunk.

"Lupita, my precious hija!" Mama grabbed her and hugged her tight. "We must all evacuate. Carlos, I'll call your parents to come pick you up."

He nodded, cradling his arm.

"Is your arm OK?" Lupita asked him, her voice shaking.

"It hurts a lot," Carlos answered, narrowing his

eyes at her. "But we have much bigger problems."

A thick, orange river of lava was moving down the volcano. More lava spewed from the top. The smell of smoke charred the air.

Lupita didn't want to believe the fire giant had erupted the volcano. It was too awful. She shut her eyes tight and shook her head. But when she opened her eyes again, the lava was still there.

Papa came out of the house, supporting Abuela who shuffled next to him. Abuela's head lifted when she saw Lupita. Her mouth opened, but no sound came out. Lupita got the feeling Abuela was desperate to tell her something. What?

"Get what you need and get in the car," Papa told Lupita.

Lupita ran into the house, Carlos on her heels.

"This is all my fault!" Lupita cried as she raced to her room. She stuffed her backpack full of random clothes, not even noticing what she grabbed. Tears flooded her eyes. "I led Nilda there."

"It's not your fault," Carlos said in a soft voice. "Let's just get out of here."

Everything felt wrong, including running away

from the fire giant.

"If I could just speak to him…" Lupita said.

"Who, the fire giant?" Carlos exclaimed. "Don't be ridiculous!"

Lupita raced into Abuela's room next, pausing to hold the doorframe as the house shook.

"Where are you going?" Carlos yelled. He braced himself on the wall with his good arm.

"Abuela's memory box," Lupita explained. "She has her most precious secrets in it." The house was probably going to be burned to ash. She had to save Abuela's things.

Lupita dove under the bed and started pulling out bags and boxes stuffed under there. She sneezed and found the old, yellow wooden box in the far corner, next to the wall.

"We can't let her precious memories burn," Lupita said, glad she found the box. Even if the eruption was all her fault, she had done one good thing. Right?

They raced out the door, Lupita clutching the box. Carlos' parents honked from across the street. Carlos crossed to their car.

"Goodbye, Carlos," Lupita yelled. "Meet you in the mountains." Both their families had relatives in the same mountain city and would evacuate there.

Carlos' mom got out of the car to hug him. Lupita saw him wince, and his mom examined his arm. Lupita blew out, hard. Carlos was in pain because of her. Guilt twisted her stomach.

Glowing, orange lava lit up the evening sky.

"This is all wrong." Lupita shook her head. "I need to make it right."

An idea sparked in her. But it was too crazy, even for Lupita. Ridiculous, as Carlos said.

She reached through the car window with a shaking hand and placed the old, yellow memory box on Abuela's lap. Abuela grabbed her arm. She gripped hard.

"Stop the lava," Abuela said, her voice a thin whisper through an almost unmoving mouth. Still, Lupita heard it.

And since it was the same as the ridiculous idea she had just had, she decided to do it. Or at least, die trying.

Chapter
Eighteen

Abuela had used her precious energy to speak. She said to stop the lava. Lupita knew what she had to do.

Fire sparks jumped in her belly. She took a deep breath to steady herself.

Her car was full. Mama was in the driver's seat with Abuela in the passenger seat. Papa and Bernardo sat in the back seat. Luggage piled in the hatchback spilled onto the little space meant for her.

"Mama," Lupita said. "Our car is full of stuff. I'll go with Carlos."

"OK, hurry," Mama said and stroked Lupita's arm through the open car window.

"See you in the mountains," Lupita said as she kissed her mom. She felt a twist in her heart. Would she ever see her family again?

Her parents pulled away and drove out of view. Lupita could change her mind. She could go with Carlos' family to safety.

She looked longingly at Carlos' car, one whole empty backseat that could be for her. But no. She had to stop the fire giant. She was the only one that could. She began to run.

She ran along the shaking street to get to the volcano. That was the only thought in her mind. But it was going to take forever to get there. Halfway down the street, a long tree branch made her stop. Would it work? Hot sparks awoke in her gut. She closed her eyes.

"Fire, I need…" she said aloud. She felt silly. Who did she think she was, trying to control fire?

Not control it, she told herself. Be its friend.

"Fire, would you please light this tree branch and fly me to the fire giant?" Lupita asked, squeezing her eyes shut and hoping hard that it worked.

The sparks in her gut combined into a ball of flickering heat. It rose up within Lupita. When the heat ball reached her throat, she blew it onto the end of the branch.

It lit. And more amazingly, the branch lifted off the ground. Lupita let out a whoop and punched the air. She did it! She used fire magic on purpose!

But there was no time to lose. The orange lava was creeping further down the volcano, already near the middle of the mountain. Lupita jumped on top of the branch.

"Wait!" Carlos' voice reached her ears. He huffed as he ran down the street towards her, cradling his arm. "I saw you leave," Carlos said. "What are you doing?" Then his gaze dropped to the hovering branch, and he froze.

"Carlos!" Lupita exclaimed, worry fizzing through her. "Go back to your car. Get to safety!"

"But where are you going?" Carlos stared at her, his mouth hanging open.

"Look, I know you don't understand," Lupita said. "But I have to try to stop the lava. Abuela thinks I can."

Carlos squeezed his eyes shut, his face ghostly under the streetlamp. His fists balled up. Then he blew out his breath and opened his eyes.

"I can't believe I am saying this," he said. "But I can't let you go alone."

"What?" Lupita blinked her eyes at Carlos. He climbed onto the branch and sat behind Lupita. His good arm tightened around her middle.

"Your arm is hurt, maybe broken!" Lupita yelled. "And your parents...won't they come after us?"

"I told my parents I was going in your car," Carlos said into her ear. "They probably drove away by now. You have to let me come."

His arm around her middle hung on tight. The smoky scent of ash carried on the breeze. There was no time to argue.

"Please fly us to the giant," Lupita asked the branch. A part of her brightened that her best friend was with her.

They zipped over the houses through the night. Carlos' head pressed into her back. She knew he'd be closing his eyes, afraid to look.

But Lupita's eyes took in the city below and the little, lit houses the size of toys. She felt the thrill of being on a flying branch, wind racing through her hair. It combined with fear as they raced towards the erupting volcano. Her whole body was electric with fiery energy.

The streets were full of cars. Headlights pointed to the mountains. Everyone was running from the volcano. Everyone except for Lupita and Carlos.

The spewing lava and the orange-red river creeping down the volcano got bigger as Lupita and Carlos neared. Lava glowed against the night.

The branch took them upwards, towards the column of smoke. Sweat filled Lupita's armpits and ran down her forehead, stinging her eyes.

The fire giant stood on top of the crater. He was enormous, as tall as the biggest building in the biggest city, and full of yellow flames. Sparks leapt off him. Would he see them?

Lupita and Carlos hovered above the fire giant's head, riding the branch. Smoke and heat stung her eyes.

"Fire giant!" Lupita yelled. She felt as small as a

firefly.

Orange eyes in a yellow flame face tilted up.

"My friend!" he roared. "Good, you are safe. I will release even more of the lava! End this city!"

"No, please!" Lupita yelled. "My family and my friends are not safe. Our homes will be destroyed."

"That is the fault of all who have forgotten me and forgotten to respect nature!" the fire giant boomed.

"You told me to make friends with fire," Lupita said. "You are not doing that. You are out of control!"

"So what?" the fire giant shouted. He threw a fireball off the mountain, which soared down like a comet.

"This is just angry fire!" Lupita said. "It is not what you want to do!"

"Are you so sure?" the fire giant asked, throwing another fireball. Lupita felt so small as she and Carlos hovered near the oven-hot head of flames. What could she possible do?

"What would your son, Queple, think?" Lupita yelled. "And your wife, under the ocean?"

"They would understand," the fire giant roared

so loud it hurt Lupita's ears.

"It's pointless," Carlos said into her ear. "It's a monster."

"He's not a monster!" Lupita yelled.

Panic raced through Lupita. She kicked her legs as she rode the branch. What could she do? Another risky idea ran through her mind. She had to try it.

"Okay, I get it," Lupita yelled even louder, to be heard above the noise of the cracking, erupting mountain. "If you want to destroy the city, go ahead!"

The fire giant's eyes met Lupita's. A fireball burned in his hand, unthrown.

"Really?" the fire giant asked.

"I just have one favor," Lupita shouted.

The fire giant nodded one slow, burning nod.

"If you're going to destroy everyone and everything, start with me."

Chapter
Nineteen

Lupita stared at the fire giant, who stared back. Carlos' thin arm tightened around her stomach. She gripped the branch, her body tight with tension.

She asked the fire giant to destroy her before the city. Would he really do it?

"I'm not afraid to die for my city," Lupita announced, holding her head high.

"I will not hurt you," the fire giant replied. "You are my friend." Yellow sparks shot off his bright body. Lupita dodged a wild flame. The branch wobbled and Carlos gasped. Lupita's heart was in her throat. They could easily fall into hot lava.

She shook her head clear of the scary thought.

She had to keep trying. She couldn't let her city burn.

"If the lava reaches my city, you will hurt me," Lupita explained. "My home will be destroyed."

"You can build a new home." His head flamed like the sun.

"My whole city will suffer!" Lupita yelled.

"That is their fault!" the fire giant roared. "Queple is not safe with those bad humans living so near!"

Something large and golden shot up from the crater, past the fire giant into the sky. Lupita felt Carlos jump. She nearly fell off the branch. Her hands grabbed on tight as her stomach somersaulted.

Queple hovered over them, a yellow-winged firebird.

"What is that?" Carlos asked.

"He's the fire giant's son," Lupita said.

The fire giant tilted his head up at Queple. The flames around the giant's heart turned orange. Lupita swore the fireball in his hand got smaller. But she couldn't be sure, because smoke was clouding her vision. She wiped her stinging eyes.

A jet of hot air bumped the branch. Suddenly, she couldn't feel Carlos' arm around her middle. Panic flooded her.

Gripping the branch with both hands, she turned. Carlos hung on to the stick with his good arm. If he fell, he would land in the hot, rolling lava.

"Help me!" Carlos yelled.

Lupita twisted to try to grab his arm, to pull him back on the branch. But she couldn't do it without losing her own balance.

"Lupita!" Carlos' panicked cry shook her. She

broke into a clammy sweat when she saw his grip slipping. She shot out a hand. But all she felt was Carlos' fingers…and then only wood.

Carlos had let go. Vomit rose in her throat as he fell towards the sea of lava.

A golden flash soared under Lupita, jolting the branch again. It rocked from side to side. Lupita had to hang on tight.

The golden flash was Queple. The fiery bird grabbed Carlos in a yellow claw just before he hit the lava. Queple flew up into the sky.

Lupita held her hand to her heart, which hammered. "He's OK, he's OK," she muttered to herself.

"The firebird saved me!" Carlos cheered. He sat in Queple's claw, his good arm around a talon. Queple hovered above Lupita, his beaky head high.

Carlos was grinning even though he held his hurt arm close to his chest. Tears flooded Lupita's cheeks. She tried to control the ocean threatening to pour from her.

"Your friend is OK," the fire giant's low, rumbling voice came to her.

"But he almost wasn't," Lupita said, her voice catching. "And my city will be destroyed and it's all my fault." Her heart felt painful, her chest light.

"How is it your fault?" the fire giant asked. "You gave me the red flower. You are a friend."

Tears and smoke made the fire giant look like a blurry mass of hot yellow.

"I brought Nilda here," Lupita explained, her voice catching. "If she hadn't thrown the can, none of this would have happened."

"I was angry before Nilda's can," the fire giant said. "I was so angry about all the other cans and trash everywhere."

"There are good humans in the city too," Lupita said, sniffling. "People who care about nature."

"You are right," the fire giant said. "If I destroy the city, I will hurt you and Carlos and all the good humans."

The rumbling and cracking of the earth stopped. Plumes of smoke became thinner as lava stopped coming out of the crater.

The fire giant tilted his head up, towards the fiery bird.

"Queple, my boy," the fire giant said with a smile. "You are a hero. You saved Lupita's friend."

Queple stretched his wings out, spreading golden flames against the night sky. Stars glimmered through tendrils of smoke.

The fire giant was calming down. Lupita wished she could be happy. But the danger was not yet over.

Lava ran all the way down to the base of the mountain. Soon it would crawl towards the city, burning everything in its path.

Chapter
Twenty

The path down the volcano was now a hot river, glowing in the night. Lava pooled into a glowing, orange, fiery lake at the base of the volcano.

As Lupita watched, the lake of lava split into two rivers, which started to crawl towards the city.

Carlos sat in Queple's golden claw. His good arm was wrapped around a talon. Even though he was safe, Lupita's heart felt tight. Their city would be destroyed. All the houses. All the beautiful trees and plants. People and creatures who hadn't made it out in time. Lupita fought to catch her breath.

"What can we do?" she cried, as the lava, brighter

than the stars, crept like giant fingers towards the houses.

The fire giant turned his head to the west. Lupita followed his gaze to the black ocean.

"Fiera will never forgive me," the fire giant said. "I destroyed so much. You helped me calm down. But it was too late. I am sorry."

Lupita's heart was a sea of tears. Was it really too late to save the city?

She looked out to the ocean, the stars like shining jewels over the black water. Wait…*water*. Water could put out fire.

"If Fiera lives under there, could she help?" Lupita asked, pointing out at the ocean. "Does she have water power?"

"She has fire power like mine," the fire giant said. "But many of her underwater friends have water power."

The great rivers of lava picked up speed. They didn't have much time left to save the city. Lupita had a wild, ridiculous idea.

Since her last ridiculous idea worked, she had some hope.

"Could Fiera erupt her underwater volcano and create a wave?" Lupita asked.

The fire giant's body danced with sudden, orange flames.

"A wave to cool the lava!" He nodded, sending sparks from his head into the night.

Carlos leaned out from Queple's claw. "You want to create a tidal wave?" Carlos said. "That sounds worse than the lava!"

"Not if Fiera's ocean friends could control the wave," Lupita said. "Direct the wave—"

"—away from the city." Carlos finished the sentence. "That sounds scary, though. What if it doesn't work?"

"The city will definitely be destroyed if we don't do anything," Lupita said. "Fire giant, can you ask Fiera what she thinks about the plan?"

"I will send Fiera a message," the fire giant said. "Water is one of the best ways to stop fire after all."

"As long as we can stop the water too," Carlos said. Queple squawked.

The fire giant scooped up a ball of hot, steaming lava from the crater. His other arm of fire reached deep into the earth and pulled out soil. He packed the soil around the red-hot ball.

"Why are you making a dirty fireball?" Carlos asked.

The fire giant didn't answer. He brought the dirt-covered fireball to his mouth and whispered. Lupita jumped as the fire giant threw back his arm and hurled the ball off the mountain. It made an arc through the air and dropped into the ocean like a flare.

"Help us, Fiera, my love," the fire giant said. He looked out to the ocean with a hand on his orange flame heart.

It was so quiet. The only sound was distant waves rushing in, rushing out. Two rivers of lava from the volcano had crossed the hills. They almost reached the first houses of the city.

Suddenly a ball of dirt shot out of the crater. Queple caught it in his beak, then dropped it in the fire giant's hand. The giant held the ball of dirt to his heart, absorbing the flames inside it.

"Fiera has erupted her volcano!" the fire giant shouted.

"Wait, we just wanted to ask her about the plan!" Lupita said, her voice coming out squeaky.

"I think it's too late for that," Carlos said in a small voice.

The fire giant chittered to Queple, who squawked back. Queple soared closer to Lupita.

"You are not safe on that tiny branch. Climb into his claw, my friend," the fire giant roared. "Do it now!"

To the west, the horizon was suddenly a wall of black. It was like a mountain had appeared, blocking all the stars.

A mountain of water.

"Did Fiera explain her plan?" Carlos asked in a shaky voice.

"She only said the wave was coming," the fire giant answered.

A minute ago, Lupita was scared lava would destroy her city. Now she prayed it wouldn't be flooded. She wrapped her hands around two of Queple's surprisingly cool, golden talons. With shaky legs, she pulled herself up to standing. It was scary to balance her feet on the flying branch.

Taking a breath to stop shaking, she pulled herself up into the claw.

It was strangely comfortable, like a soft but firm armchair. Carlos gave her a thumbs-up from the other claw.

The tidal wave moved fast. More stars disappeared from the sky as it got closer, taller. Her stomach somersaulted.

"The wave will cool the lava and stop its flow," the fire giant explained, watching the dark water wall approach. "But there will be much steam! Queple must fly you to safety."

Queple flapped his huge, shining wings. Wind ruffled Lupita's hair as they headed west.

"Wait, the water is dangerous for you too!" Lupita yelled to the fire giant. But they were flying fast across the water, and she didn't think he could hear.

"Queple, we need to help your papa if we can," Lupita said. "Don't take us so far!"

"Somewhere far sounds good to me," Carlos argued from his claw.

Queple's great wings flapped slower. Lupita felt

her stomach drop as Queple flew in a great arc to change direction. The great, fiery bird flew back to the volcano, climbing high in the sky. He hovered in the stars.

"Queple, thank you!" Lupita shouted.

From high up, the volcano looked like a small, dark mountain with streaks of red-orange lava. The air was cooler up here. She shivered when she saw the tidal wave. It was nearly at the mountain.

"I know you don't like him," Lupita explained to Carlos. "But I don't want the fire giant to be hurt." She imagined her fiery friend dowsed with ocean water and tears came.

"He's not so bad," Carlos said from Queple's other claw. "And he seems like a smart fire giant. He'll be OK."

They were too far apart to hold hands, but Lupita felt his closeness anyway. It soothed her heart.

Then the wave hit.

123

Chapter
Twenty-one

Even from high up in Queple's claw, Lupita could hear the huge wave when it hit the volcano. Crashing water met rock. It roared and sizzled. She gripped Queple's talon tighter.

The wave was as tall as the volcano. Taller.

Steam covered the volcano and rose into the night. The fuzzy cloud below Lupita hid the mountain top.

Queple flapped even higher. Lupita was sticky with sweat, and the cold air felt refreshing. It would be nice up here if she wasn't so worried about the fire giant. And her city.

Past the steam cloud, the city was dark. Hopefully that meant everyone had left.

But the trees, the flowers, deer in the hills, all the cats…what about them? Would they be burned by lava? Drowned in the tidal wave?

She closed her eyes and sent a wish that everyone, all the life, would be safe.

Queple dropped to the edge of the steam cloud near the city. He beat his massive wings towards the steam.

"He's blowing the steam cloud out to the ocean!" Carlos called from the other talon.

"Clever Queple," Lupita called back, hoping the fiery bird could hear her praise.

Queple kept moving his wings until the steam cloud disappeared. The volcano was black against the night. The color of cool, hard lava.

The moon was rising. A lake had formed in the dry hills between the volcano and the city. It shimmered in silvery blue. A wide river ran into the city from the lake.

Lupita's throat was tight as she studied the landscape.

"Can you see how much of the city is flooded?" Lupita called to Carlos.

"That river looks pretty bad to me," Carlos said.

Queple soared lower. Lupita could see the water more clearly now.

The big lake by the volcano's base was getting smaller. Two rivers were draining the lake back into the ocean. Lupita blinked in surprise as a tail fin splashed out of the lake. A woman's face appeared, her long hair gleaming in the moonlight. Another tail fin glinted, and a man with starfish in his hair waved up at them.

Queple chittered.

"Mermaids are real?" Carlos asked.

"I guess so!" Lupita said. "Look, they are saving the animals!"

Two mermaids swam together, pushing a deer out of the lake. The deer stumbled onto shore.

Another mermaid with five cats riding her got close to shore. The cats all jumped off, hissed at each other and ran into the bush. Lupita's heart sang to see the animals were alive.

Queple soared just above the volcano. The

crater was much bigger now.

"Where is the fire giant?" Lupita asked. The crater was dark and there were no yellow sparks. No orange eyes.

Queple hovered just over a ledge below the crater. Lupita climbed out of the claw and jumped to solid ground. She placed her hands on the cool, black earth. Lava turned to stone.

Carlos dropped too, landing on his knees and good arm. He cradled his hurt one.

"Now that we are safe, it hurts more," he complained, wincing.

Queple dipped his head. His beak was over Carlos' elbow. Lupita watched, amazed, as a moonlit tear formed from Queple's eye. Queple blinked and the tear dropped like silvery watercolor paint onto Carlos' elbow.

"Wow!" Lupita exclaimed.

"My arm feels better – like magic," Carlos said.

He rolled his shoulder and flexed his arm, waggling his fingers.

"It's fixed!" he yelled with a huge grin. "It doesn't even hurt."

Queple gave a mighty squawk.

"You're the best firebird ever!" Carlos said. Queple straightened up even more. His beak curved up. Was he smiling?

A familiar voice came from above them, from the crater.

"Queple, you have saved my friends," the fire giant said. His enormous, flaming head popped out of the crater. Giant eyes peered down at Carlos, Lupita and Queple.

"You're OK!" Lupita said, her face breaking into a grin.

"I covered myself with dirt, to hide from the water," he explained.

"I am so glad you are alive," Lupita gushed. "The city might be flooded. We don't know how bad it is yet."

She wondered if her house was all right. What about the garden, and Nayeli's ancient bush with red flowers?

At least her family was safe.

"Our families will be so worried about us," Carlos lamented, his arms crossed against his stomach.

"They don't know we're still alive."

"Can Queple take us to the mountains?" Lupita asked the fire giant. She hoped Queple could fly over their house on the way.

The fire giant gazed at Lupita.

"Ask my son yourself," the fire giant answered. "He is old enough to make his own decisions now."

Lupita and Carlos looked at the fiery bird. Queple nodded his head, his beak curving low.

"Thank you," Lupita said.

The fire giant pulled out a dirt ball the size of a basketball from the crater. It was red clay…the color of fire.

"Queple, can you take this seed ball?" the fire giant asked. "If you drop it in Lupita's garden, she can use her fire power to make the special red flowers grow."

Queple took the dirt ball in his claw from the fire giant's hand.

"Was Nayeli's bush a gift from you?" Lupita asked.

"It was from the fire giant before me," he said. "Please grow the red flowers again if your garden is flooded."

"Thank you," Lupita said, her heart warm. "And we will not forget to bring them to you every year."

The fire giant's heart flames grew orange. "Do you forgive me for erupting the volcano?" the fire giant asked in a low voice.

"Of course I do," Lupita said. "Friends forgive each other."

"Lupita, thank you for teaching me to be a friend," the fire giant said. "I haven't had a human friend since Nayeli. You reminded me how wonderful humans can be."

"And you taught me how wonderful fire giants are," Lupita said. "All of them." She gazed up at Queple, who was patiently waiting nearby, holding the dirt ball with the special seeds in it.

"I will go to Fiera," the fire giant said. "I can finally be with her, under the ocean."

"I thought you said you couldn't leave Queple," Lupita said. "That it wasn't safe."

"Queple has proven he can take care of himself," he said. "And he has good friends."

The fire giant smiled at Lupita, orange flames

rushing out of his mouth and forming the shape of a heart in the air.

A swirl of emotions moved through Lupita. Her shoulders were heavy with exhaustion and her eyes teared up.

"I will miss you," she said. If the fire giant was under the ocean, would she ever see him again?

"I will visit," the fire giant promised. Queple cawed, and the sound spread throughout the sky.

"Let's go," Carlos said.

Chapter
Twenty-two

Lupita and Carlos climbed into Queple's claw. They each held onto a talon. It was nice to be in the same claw together. She hoped Carlos felt the same way.

Lupita wasn't sure Carlos forgave her yet.

The seed ball in Queple's other claw gave Lupita hope. Even if their garden was flooded, the magic red flowers would still be able to grow.

"Are we friends again?" Lupita asked Carlos in a small voice as the great, fiery bird took them into the sky.

"Of course," Carlos said. "Friends forgive each other. Though if you are hiding another fire giant from me…" he knotted his eyebrows together.

"I promise, no more secrets," Lupita said.

"Also, you're not totally forgiven until you give me…" He counted his fingers. "Ten desserts."

"OK, that's fair," she said, though her chest felt tight. So, she wasn't yet forgiven.

"And I will give you ten desserts in return," he said with a grin.

"Even fairer," Lupita replied, her face relaxing into a soft smile.

They flew away from the ocean, the moon shining down like a silver lamp. It was beautiful, but Lupita felt heavy inside. Moonlight reflected off flooded streets. Yards, driveways were underwater.

"At least the mermaids saved the animals," Carlos said, squeezing Lupita's shoulder. She leaned against him.

Lupita directed Queple to her garden. It looked like a pond. Nayeli's bush was underwater. Only one fir tree rose up from the flooding. She hoped it would survive.

Queple dropped the seed ball at the edge of the pond, in the corner of the garden next to the house. Lupita connected with the sparks in the dirt and asked politely if they would grow. Warmth from her heart ran into her hands. She sent the heat towards the flower seeds.

"I see golden light coming from your hands," Carlos said, his arm around Lupita's shoulder. "Your fire power is officially awesome."

"And under control," she agreed, feeling a weight lift off her shoulders.

Queple soared higher and carried them towards the mountains. Now they just had to face their parents. They could never explain what had happened.

"What will we say?" Lupita asked Carlos.

His face turned stony with fear, and he shrugged. Lupita felt the same alarm through her.

"We'll figure it out together," Carlos promised. Lupita's stomach knotted tightly as the mountains grew bigger.

Chapter
Twenty-three

A week later, Lupita stood in the garden while her parents unpacked the car. They were finally back from the mountains. They had to stay a week because of the flooded roads. In that week, Lupita slept a lot. She and Carlos stayed silent about what really happened. She knew Mama would ask her about it again, though. How could she explain?

The garden had dried out a little. Instead of a pond, it was a mud pit. The fir tree had survived. All the other plants and flowers were dead, except the new bush by Abuela's window.

"Where did that bush come from?" Mama asked

as she picked her way over to Lupita in her heels. Her shoes sank into the mud and she frowned.

Lupita didn't answer. She sucked her cheeks in.

"So you're not going to tell me anything," Mama complained. "Really, nothing at all."

Lupita stared at her dirt-streaked sneakers. She knew Mama would never believe her about the fire giant. Or Queple, or the mermaids who saved the city from the tidal wave. So she said nothing.

Besides, she and Carlos had made a pact. They could not reveal Queple to anyone. Only Abuela.

"You said you would tell me what happened when we got back from the mountains," Mama said, a hand on her hip. "Well, now we're back."

"I can't," Lupita mumbled.

"Well, we've spoken to Carlos' parents," Mama continued. "If you don't tell us what happened, you are both grounded for two months."

A flood of warmth shot through Lupita's face. She opened her mouth to complain. Then she swallowed the heat and closed her lips. What could she say?

It wasn't fair. She and Carlos had risked their lives to save the city. But they couldn't tell anyone.

Abuela's window was cracked open. She was the only one who would understand. But Abuela had been in bed since the journey to the mountains, exhausted. So Lupita hadn't been able to tell her what happened.

Mama's cell phone rang. Probably another neighbor. Her phone was ringing nonstop.

Lupita studied the bush and felt a glow in her belly. She would give it some more warm fire energy later, to help it grow. Lupita hoped she could pick a special red flower soon. There were already buds on the bush.

"All the cats and the dogs are OK?" Mama was saying into her cell phone. "It is strange. How did they survive the flooding?"

Lupita's heart warmed as she remembered the cats being carried to safety by mermaids.

"True," Mama said. "A tidal wave could have flooded us all the way to the attic. Who knows why so much of the water missed us."

Lupita felt a smile curl on her lips. The memory

of a mermaid with a starfish in her hair popped into her mind. She had waved from one of the rivers, bringing water back from land into the ocean. The flooding could have been so much worse.

The next call was from the furniture store. Though the stone tiles in the kitchen would dry out, all the rugs on the ground floor had to be replaced.

"Can I go to my room?" Lupita asked, interrupting the call.

"No, mi hija, stay out here with me," Mama said. But she didn't look angry. Her eyes were soft as she put away the phone. "You know when you disappeared, when you and Carlos didn't come to the mountains, I feared the worst."

Lupita nodded slowly. She didn't like to think how worried her family had been.

"Your great-great-grandmother Nayeli had a strange connection with the volcano," Mama whispered. "Some people called her a witch. It has always been a dark secret in our family."

Lupita tensed. What did Mama know?

"Well, I think I am like Nayeli," Lupita admitted. "And I think the secret is not dark but very bright."

Mama stared at her, her brown eyes large under heavy mascara.

"No, you are not like Nayeli," Mama said. "You are just you. I am very glad you are safe."

"I'm sorry Carlos and I scared you," Lupita told her, with a steady gaze. "We had to help. That is all I can say."

"If you can't tell me what happened, it is OK," Mama soothed. "I don't understand the volcano like you do. Like Nayeli did."

Mama pulled her into a hug.

"Does this mean we're not grounded?" Lupita asked, hopefully, held in Mama's arms.

"You are most certainly grounded for worrying us," Mama answered, squeezing tighter.

Lupita sighed. She didn't know what Mama thought had happened. But she guessed she was forgiven.

Even though she was still grounded for two months.

Chapter
Twenty-four

School was finally dry enough to reopen. Lupita stepped into history class with a plan.

Mr. Gonzalez explained how lava cooled in the water, turning to black stone. How fire and water made land.

She barely paid attention to the lecture. She had been there and seen it for herself anyway.

Lupita had an old photo in her pocket. It came from Abuela's yellow memory box. At the end of class, she showed the photo to Mr. Gonzalez.

"How wonderful, I haven't seen this photo before," he said, his gaze on the woman in the fringed shawl at the top of the volcano.

"It's my ancestor Nayeli," Lupita explained. "She is about to lay a red flower near the crater to honor it."

"You look a lot like her," he commented, his eyes flicking back and forth between Lupita and the photo.

"I feel connected to her, and to the flower and corn ceremony," Lupita explained. "I was just thinking…"

Her throat was suddenly dry. Would Mr. Gonzalez find her idea too strange?

She focused on the fire power warming her belly, and silently asked it to help her. Hot strength flooded through her, breaking through her shyness.

"I think we should honor the volcano too," Lupita explained, her voice strong. "The flowers grow in my garden."

"Garden plants didn't survive the flooding," Mr. Gonzalez pointed out, frowning.

"This special bush did," Lupita explained, giving him a bright smile.

"Well, someone is watching over it then," he

said, his eyebrows raised. "Maybe Nayeli."

"Maybe," Lupita replied. She was happy to be like her ancestor. In more than one way.

Lupita hopped back to her desk, where Carlos waited for her. She smiled big as she told Carlos about the plans to honor the volcano, and honor Queple. The best part was, they could go even if they were grounded. It was a school trip.

And she had lunch money to spend. Nilda had left the classroom without looking at Lupita once.

"Is it my turn to share dessert, or yours?" Lupita asked.

"Let's both get dessert and swap," he replied, smiling. She and Carlos left for the canteen, arms linked together.

Chapter
Twenty-five

The school bus parked at the base of the volcano. Lupita's class was loud and noisy as everyone rushed out. The sounds rattled Lupita's brain and angry fire sparks jumped inside her. But she knew how to cool them now. She breathed deep.

Lupita took red flowers from her basket and placed them in each of her classmate's hands. Mr. Gonzalez took one too, with a smile. Only Nilda refused, crossing her arms and leaning against the bus.

After Carlos handed out the ears of corn, he hooked his elbow through Lupita's. Together, they led the class up the cool, dry lava path. Broken, black trees stood on either side. It was such a sad sight. But Mr. Gonzalez told them new trees would grow. They just had to be patient.

Her classmates became quiet as they climbed up the path. Lupita looked back and noticed everyone was holding their red flower and corn carefully. She felt a wave of hope that maybe her classmates would honor the volcano for real.

When they got to the top, there were gasps. Lupita felt her heart jump too. The crater was enormous, bigger than before the eruption. Tendrils of smoke curled from it. Lupita guessed the smoke was from Queple, resting in the volcano.

She knew the fire giant was with Fiera, in her volcano under the ocean. It made Lupita's heart feel full, knowing that her friend was with his love.

They couldn't climb any closer to the crater. They lay the flowers and corn just below it. Each flower was a splash of cheerful red on the black ground.

"Thank you," Lupita called, and others began to say their own words.

"We love you," one girl said to the volcano.

"Please don't erupt," another girl spoke.

"We won't litter anymore," a boy promised.

"Queple, see you soon," Carlos called.

"From me too, Queple," she called. No one would understand what they meant, so she felt safe to say it.

The ride back on the bus was quiet, until someone mentioned lunch. Then the noise climbed to volcano erupting level.

Lupita didn't mind this time. She laughed along with her classmates as someone described an exploding enchilada. Carlos shyly wondered aloud what exploding flan would look like.

When she got home, she didn't care that she was grounded. The smells of Mama's cooking came from the kitchen.

"Enchiladas after your homework's done," Mama called.

"Great!" Lupita answered, a laugh escaping her. Hopefully they wouldn't be exploding ones.

"Oh, and here," Mama said, handing her a plate of fruit. "To help fuel your homework."

Lupita smiled. After the walk up the volcano, the

fruit was delicious. Not only did she eat lunch these days, she got snacks too. Life was getting better. If only she could talk to Abuela. Then everything would be back to normal. Even better than normal.

Abuela had her eyes closed in the hammock. Lupita touched her ancient, bony hand that was also so soft.

A turn in her heart made her wonder if Abuela would just keep sleeping and resting now. She hadn't joined the family for meals at all, just ate soup quietly in her room. Could Lupita ever tell her the story of how she, Carlos, Queple and the fire giant worked together to save the city?

That night, after enchiladas with her family, Lupita fell asleep with a full belly and a peaceful smile.

Suddenly, in her dream, she was outside under huge, winking stars like diamonds. She stood on the path just below the crater, and Queple soared above—a bright, golden bird. Two soft, bony hands slipped around hers. Lupita looked up at the old, wrinkled face and smiled.

"An Abuela hand-sandwich," Lupita whispered

in her dream.

Abuela nodded, her dark eyes full of secrets and love.

"Do you know what happened?" Lupita asked her.

Abuela touched her own heart, then Lupita's heart. A softness entered Lupita's other hand. It was a red flower.

Abuela leaned close and Lupita leaned down to hear.

"I see you," Abuela whispered in a scratchy, thin voice.

Lupita felt warmth fill her like golden flames. Abuela had a red flower too. They linked hands and lay their flowers by the crater at the same time.

When Lupita woke up, she knew that Abuela would always be with her. So would Nayeli. And every time she offered a red flower to the volcano, she would remember them.

About the
Author

Giulietta M Spudich loves to travel and experience different cultures and lands. Half-Italian, American with a home in Cambridge, England, she's a mix of cultures herself. A nature-lover, she writes middle grade fantasies connecting with the elements. The Fire Giant is her sixth book with Handersen Publishing. Find Giulietta on Twitter @spudichpen and on FaceBook @GiuliettaBooks

Discover more at:
www.ElementGirls.org

Acknowledgements
And Thank You's

Nicki and Tevin at Handersen Publishing. I love Nicki's cover design and thanks for all the other hidden work she does like layout and herding cats. A big thanks to the rest of Team Fire Giant. Lewis, Alejandra and Jeff, I especially appreciate all the help bringing Mexico to life with excellent suggestions about the cultural habits and history of the region...and, of course, the delicious foods! Also a big thanks to my young test readers, Amber and Mika, who provided enthusiasm for an earlier draft. Enthusiasm goes a long way in working through rounds of revisions to get to the final copy. Thanks to the Scholars Walkers for help with a very early draft. And huge gratitude to my brother John. I love his vision of Queple, especially. The book has a fuller story due to his dynamic illustrations. Gratitude to the excellent teachers at the Golden Egg Academy, and for all I've learned on their young fiction writing course. And thanks to all you readers for getting to know Lupita and the Fire Giant. And all those litter pickers out there, the world needs you!

Thank you for purchasing and reading *The Fire Giant*. Handersen Publishing is an independent publishing house that specializes in creating quality young adult, middle grade, and picture books.

We hope you enjoyed this book and will consider leaving a review on Goodreads or Amazon. A small review can make a big difference. Thank you.

"The author has done such a wonderful job of making Clarissa's challenges just a preamble to the real story of a young girl who is able to find good in all places and is brave enough to stand for what she knows is right, despite how difficult it gets for her."

-5 stars, Amazon Review

Also by Giulietta M. Spudich
The Giant Series

A unique story to take your children out of their everyday world.

"The Amber Giant is an inspirational story for children and pre-teens that combines adventure, learning, and lessons in kindness and friendship. It's a captivating, highly creative read that will mesmerize your children with a unique plotline that will take them out of their everyday world. A fun story for adults too! I highly recommend."

-5 stars, Amazon Customer Review

A whimsical adventure that promotes individuality and self-acceptance.

-Kirkus Review

"Lovely inter-generation story starring moody, 13-year old Elika. She's finding her place in the world, in her family and finding out what's important to her. Great to read a book featuring strong female characters who form a supportive and interesting family lineage (daughter, mother, aunt, and features memories of grandma)."

-5 stars, Goodreads Review

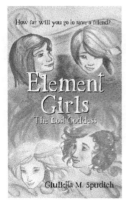

Ingram Content Group UK Ltd.
Milton Keynes UK
UKHW041040210623
423798UK00005B/107